Ghosts of PERRY HOUSE

CC BROWN

Ghosts of Perry House, Copyright © 2021 by CC Brown

Published by: Home Grown Books

Layout by Judi Fennell at www.formatting4U.com

All rights reserved.
Ghosts of Perry House is a work of fiction. Apart from the well-known actual people, events, and locations that figure in the narrative, all names, characters, places, and incidents are the product of the author's imagination. Any resemblance to current events or locales, persons living or dead, is entirely coincidental.

No part of this publication may be reproduced, distributed, or transmitted in any form or by any means, including photocopying, recording, or other electronic or mechanical methods, or by any information storage and retrieval system without the prior written permission of the publisher, except in the case of very brief quotations embodied in critical reviews and certain other noncommercial uses permitted by copyright law.

About the Authors

CC Brown is the pseudonym adopted by the two sisters Schyrlet Cameron and Kathy Brown. Growing up in the Ozarks their curiosity about the supernatural was sparked by their grandmother. As children, much of their time was spent on their grandparent's farm, where she always kept them entertained... tending the garden, feeding the chickens, milking the cows, and telling deliciously spooky late-night tales. Their fascination with ghosts and spirits from beyond the grave has not diminished over time.

Forward
A Haunted Hotel
Eureka Springs, Arkansas

The 1905 Basin Park Hotel is one of Arkansas' real haunted hotels. The hotel has long been the source of eerie tales, unusual happenings, and many ghostly encounters. According to town history, by 1880, an elegant, four-story hotel known as the Perry House was built on the site of the healing springs which gives Eureka its name. Eureka Springs grew rapidly because of the spring water. The "healing waters" attracted the rich and those looking to get rich. Gambling, drinking, and prostitution were popular activities available at the seventeen saloons in operation. Many notorious outlaws were drawn to the boomtown including Frank and Jessie James, the Younger brothers, Belle Starr, and members of the Dalton Gang.

Like most other buildings in Eureka Springs at that time, the Perry House Hotel was built completely out of wood. In 1890, it fell victim to the last of the four fires that completely leveled the town of Eureka Springs. William Duncan built the Basin Park Hotel from local limestone in 1905, on the site of the old Perry House. Duncan died in 1907, but it's believed that he continues to roam the halls of the Basin Park Hotel in a brown suit and derby.

Besides William Duncan, there are legends about visitors who checked into the hotel, but who also never really left. Patrons in rooms 307, 308, and 310 repeatedly report sightings and encounters with a young translucent woman with blue eyes and golden-blonde hair; a little girl with braided hair in a yellow dress; and a man in a cowboy hat and white canvas duster, with

Ghosts of Perry House

a six-shooter strapped to his hip. The cowboy is said to walk through the walls of the rooms on the third floor asking startled guests if they have seen his horse. Stories involving floating orbs, moving objects, and late-night unfounded shouts of "Fire!" are frequently reported to hotel management.

Many believe the cowboy to be John Chisum, a wealthy cattle baron in the American West during the mid-to-late 19th century. It is reported Chisum came to the Basin Park Hotel to recover from surgery but died in 1884 on Christmas Eve. In our fictitious telling of the story, we imagined an alternative explanation to the identity of the cowboy. Based on the history of the Ozarks during the late 1800s and the lawlessness of the area, we believe it is possible the cowboy could have been a man on the wrong side of the law. As with Chisum, our cowboy seeks a cure from the healing waters of Eureka Springs.

Ghosts of Perry House was inspired by the mysterious and unexplainable events we experienced during our recent stay at the 1905 Basin Park Hotel. In writing our story, we tried to stay true to the history of the area and the historic hotel. We focused on facts and true incidents that have occurred. While in several instances the actual names and locations of people and businesses have been used, the facts surrounding the actual people and occurrences have been embellished. We personally look forward to revisiting the town of "healing waters" and the historic hotel to further investigate the spirits of the paranormal kind.

The Lawless Ozarks
1855-1890

The Ozark Mountain region, referred to by the locals as "the Ozarks," includes portions of Arkansas, Kansas, Missouri, and Oklahoma. Key historical events had a major impact on the lives of people living in the four-state area.

1855-Kansas Border Wars

The Border Wars, also known as "Bleeding Kansas" and "Bloody Kansas," were a series of violent conformations between settlers and pro-slavery "border ruffians." At the core of the conflict was the question of whether the Kansas Territory would allow or outlaw slavery and enter the Union as a slave state or a free state.

1856 to 1896-The Great Cattle Drives

Cattle drives were a major economic activity in the 19th and early 20th century. During these years, cowboys, many just young boys, rounded up and slowly drove millions of longhorns north from Texas to railheads in Kansas, Missouri, and Arkansas.

1861 to 1865-Civil War

The Ozarks, ravaged by both the Union and Confederate armies, was a violent and dangerous place during the four years of the Civil War. The Ozarks in southern Missouri and northern Arkansas was especially hard-hit by the Civil War. The region was sparsely populated, making it a good home for ex-guerrilla fighters from both sides as well as bandits and outlaws.

1865 to1890-Outlaws and Lawmen

The years following the Civil War were a troubling time for the Ozarks. The war brought men to the area that had learned to live by the gun. Outlaws like Jesse and Frank James and the Younger brothers became folk heroes. A few men like James Hickok and Wyatt Earp went on to use their guns to enforce the law.

1883 to 1889-Bald Knobbers

The Bald Knobbers, a gang of vigilantes, ruled the lawless post-Civil War Ozark Mountain region. The Bald Knobbers, who for the most part had sided with the North in the American Civil War, were opposed by the Anti-Bald Knobbers, who for the most part had sided with the Confederates.

Perry House Hotel 1890

Courtesy of Eureka Springs Historical Museum

Ghosts of Perry House

Life and death are one thread, the same line viewed from different sides.

> Lao Tzu

Prologue
Eureka Springs, Arkansas–1890

A lone rider traversed the winding trail of the Ozark hillside. Half-hidden in the vast hardwood forest, he rode around hastily built wooden shanties and pitched tents. Summer's late afternoon stirred the song of cicadas marking the end of a difficult day's journey. At last, horse and rider descended into the narrow valley on the main road leading to Eureka Springs, Arkansas.

Travelers on horseback, others in wagons and buggies, now shared the dirt-packed avenue with him. Many were seeking a miracle in the healing waters of one of the sixty-five natural flowing springs located in and around the city. Newspaper testimonials credited the "liquid cure" with amazing healing feats. As word of the miraculous waters began to spread, the afflicted flocked to Eureka Springs in such numbers that the town had transformed from an isolated wilderness to a flourishing city in just a few short months. He was skeptical about the miracles, but perhaps a spring bath would ease his minor injury.

The settlement was abuzz with excitement and activity. He maneuvered his new mount, a young chestnut gelding to the cedar hitching rail outside the Silver Palace Saloon. His face, weathered by a lifetime of hard living, appeared dangerous and uncaring. Casting a glance skyward and silently cursing the sizzling afternoon heat, he surveyed the unfamiliar surroundings. Women, some with children in tow or accompanied by men, strolled the walkways. Dominated by whitewashed wooden structures, the boomtown boasted a restaurant, dry goods store, blacksmith and livery, a couple of hotels, and a bank constructed of brick. Good citizens of the town had seen fit to erect a church and barbershop at one end of the street and a newspaper and post office at the other. Upstanding businessmen of Eureka Springs had not forgotten to provide accommodations pandering to the darker tastes of men of his persuasion. Next to the Silver Palace, was Miss Turnbottom's brothel and further down the street a gambling hall.

Riding by the sheriff's office, he was quick to note the collection of wanted posters tacked to the wooden planks. Relieved not to find his likeness, he reasoned the Dodge City Peace Commission had not yet issued a warrant after the deadly gunplay that had left his right arm in need of attention.

After dismounting, he wrapped the reins around the hitch. He removed the salt-stained blackened Stetson, revealing a full head of curly golden hair. A red bandana wiped beading sweat and fresh trail dust from his sun-darkened face. He smiled at the thought of easing his thirst with good whiskey. He winced in pain as he shed the light canvas duster. It was a tolerable pain; one he hoped would mend in time.

His thoughts were interrupted. "Need your horse stabled, Mister?" the young boy asked.

"Make sure he gets feed and water." The boy pocketed two-bits and led the gelding to the nearby livery.

A din of merrymaking rolled out into the street. Bawdy bar tunes echoed from a saloon piano, and shrill laughter from the whores turned into shrieks as a fight erupted and tumbled onto the main street. Another smile swept across the man's face as he cleared the three steps leading to the saloon. This would be the first stop. Dull the pain and cozy up to a fine-looking woman of the establishment.

Gun holstered low on his right hip; the smell of sweat, stale beer, and cheap perfume hit him as he gave the batwing doors an inward push. Curious heads turned. Sensing the newcomer posed no immediate threat, they went back to telling lies and swilling liquor.

He scanned the high-quality establishment. In the far-right corner, the piano player pounded out another lively tune. Painted ladies decked out in lace and fringe danced with men starved for female companionship. On the left, an enormous bar spanned half the room. Two bartenders dressed in black vests with matching bow ties stood ready to accommodate the booted and spurred trail-hands. Saloon girls, arms and shoulders bare, bodices cut low over ample bosoms, stood talking to men—enticing them to remain, buying drinks, and patronizing the games.

Striding to the bar, his left arm was nestled by the breasts of a saloon girl. A river of dark red hair streamed down her back.

"Welcome to the Silver Palace,

Cowboy. How 'bout a drink and a table?" she asked with an inviting look.

"Yes, Ma'am, a table in the back would suit me just fine."

Following his request, the young woman led him to a table. From habit, he sat with his back to a wall, facing the door to avoid getting surprised by someone looking to dispense their own version of frontier justice.

"Bottle of your best whiskey and a glass, two glasses if you care to join me," he invited.

The brazen-faced redhead, practicing the world's oldest profession, said, "Perhaps later, I've customers to tend to now."

With a wink and a nod, he said, "I sure am thirsty, Ma'am, don't know 'bout later."

"Don't wait too long!" she warned, twirling away from the table. Under the ruffled skirt, the colorful petticoats that barely reached her leather boots were visible. He caught a glimpse of silk stockings held up by garters, which he reasoned were gifts from her admirers. With an exaggerated swaying of ample hips, she weaved a trail to the bar.

Taking out tobacco pouch and papers, he rolled and lit a cigarette. His steel-gray eyes coldly took in the rest of the saloon from behind a cloud of exhaled smoke. Faro and poker players were stationed at one of the three large tables in the center of the room. Small round tables, like the one he sat at, were scattered throughout and occupied by groups of two or three men engaged in conversation. He didn't recognize anyone, and no one recognized him.

Minutes later, his drink was served. "Here ya go," she said, placing the bottle and glass in front of him.

The man used his left hand to pull three bills from his shirt pocket. "Keep the change." He poured himself a drink.

"Thanks," she beamed, "anything else, Darlin'?"

Shaking his head, no, he waved her

away. Large hips… red hair, she wasn't his type, and he didn't want or need the distraction.

Sunlight streaked through the fog of tobacco smoke as he sucked down the amber contents of the glass. He opened his mouth and let out a breath as the slow burn of the liquor washed away the dust.

He sat silently, drinking and watching the rapidly dimming afternoon sky filled with dark, roiling clouds. Forked lightning, brilliant and white-hot, flashed through the blackening heavens. Crackling thunder rippled; the deafening noise engulfed the wooden building. The storm broke with a hard rain pelting the mountain top town, bouncing off roofs, forming puddles while he carefully weighed his next steps: search the secret tunnels buried deep beneath the town, find the gold, and then head west to Oregon Country.

At the end of the day, the storm finally blew itself out. Alert but feeling the whiskey, the handsome drifter stepped out

Ghosts of Perry House

into the blue tinge of twilight. Saloon doors creaked quietly behind. Under the cover of darkness, dodging mud holes, he walked a short distance to the Perry House, a four-story hotel complete with white-columned balconies on the second and third floors. A sign on the glass front entry door read "Vacancy." Glancing back at the deserted street, his eyes scanned the shadows as his right hand instinctively tapped the pearl-handled Colt. Safety assured, he turned back and stepped into the cool sanctuary of the hotel lobby.

Chapter 1
Present

Black clouds blotted out the setting sun as the Moneyland tour bus navigated the serpentine road leading to Eureka Springs, Arkansas. Ancient oaks lined the bluffs forming a naturally arched tunnel. Trees commanded by the powerful winds lost hold of their leaves. Snapped limbs whirled through the air littering the roadway. Caught in nature's wrath, the bus driver, unfamiliar with the route, death gripped the wheel and prayed for a place to pull over. Prayers unanswered, trapped in a stormy nightmare, he fought to keep the bus on the highway as he slowed to descend the dangerously steep grade.

"Bingo!" echoed up and down the

dimly lit aisle and ricocheted off bus windows. The five-letter word brought a chorus of good-natured moans and groans from the losers. The winner screamed her excitement and waved the lucky card.

A strong gust of wind rocked the bus. The bingo official staggered to the back to confirm the numbers. Fighting to stay upright, she accidentally bumped Nicole's elbow sending her paranormal romance to the floor. "What the…?" Nicole grumbled, retrieving her new, but now scuffed paperback. She tossed the book to Kat, her sister, then stood, turned, and knelt in the seat peering over the headrest. The silhouettes were vigorously fanning themselves with their worthless cards. It was obvious; the air conditioning system couldn't crank out enough cool air to keep up with the extreme July heat.

Lightning flicked repeatedly like a reporter's camera at the premiere of a much-anticipated horror movie. In that violent illumination, Nicole saw concern growing in the eyes and actions of the other traveling tourists. Some, visibly shaken by the severity of the storm, stared wide-eyed, bracing themselves for the next round. Others chattered nervously about no cell phone reception while a few, unconcerned with the weather, cleared their pull-down tables, anticipating the next bingo game. Her friend, Mariah, in the row directly behind, fell into the last category. "Let the good times roll!" Mariah yelled, reveling in the chaos and excitement, impatiently swiping at the dark threads of unruly hair tickling her face.

Again, lightning flashed, and passengers shrieked. Nicole heard Kat counting, "*One-Mississippi, two-Mississippi, three-Mississippi.*" A method she always used to gauge the closeness of a storm. Then the thunder cracked. A quick mental calculation told Kat the strike was close. She looked at Nicole. "That was less than a mile."

Finding everyone's reaction including Kat's overly theatrical and verging on hysterical, Nicole hollered, "People, it's just a thunderstorm!" Disgusted, she plopped back into her seat.

Nicole gathered sticky blonde strands and pulled them through a hair tie from her wrist. As she whirled in her seat, the soggy ponytail lashed her sister in the face. "What in the world were you thinking?" she demanded, turning to her sister.

"Ouch!" Kat yelped, grabbing her stinging cheek. "Actually, right now, I'm thinking about snatching you bald-headed," she ground out between clenched teeth.

Realizing what she had done, Nicole quickly came back with, "I'd like to say I'm sorry, but I'm not. You deserved that and more!" Her sapphire-blue eyes shot daggers.

Blinking green eyes, feigning innocence, Kat mockingly smoothed her sleek chin-length, auburn bob before answering, "Hey, I have no control over the weather or AC. My hair loves the heat and humidity."

Ghosts of Perry House

"Cut the CRAP, Katherine Lynette!" Nicole resorted to using Kat's full name to emphasize her annoyance. "You know perfectly well what I'm talking about! I told you this morning there was a storm alert for Northern Arkansas and didn't want to take the bus! Did you listen? Hell, no!" She stopped the rant as it reached a crescendo.

Kat hated it when her sister used her given name. "Brother, you're impossible to please!" Kat shot back, fidgeting with her black-framed designer glasses as they slid down her nose. Pushing them back in place, she explained, "I saw the ad for the travel agency while cruising the Internet, *Take the bus, earn a few bucks, and leave the driving to us.* It seemed a perfect fit for our weekend retreat: daubing for dollars, spa treatments, sightseeing…"

Kat's explanation was interrupted by an explosion of blue-white forked lightning striking the bus. A blast like a sonic boom shook the earth. The interior lights flipped off and on, and then complete darkness. Startled, some folks cried out in terror; others loudly voiced their opinion of Moneyland Tours and their driver.

Right on cue, the rain fell. It came in waves, hammering the windows, splattering the pavement, and silencing the protests. Swoosh of wipers and hiss of tires amplified. Torrential rains, driven by the wind, caused the bus to hydroplane. The rear end began to veer to the left crossing the double-yellow centerline. Cries of alarm were muffled by the kettledrum rumble overhead. Panicking, the driver jerked the wheel, sending bingo cards flying and launching one startled passenger from his seat.

"Slow down!" someone yelled.

"Help! He's trying to kill us," a silver-headed senior squawked in distress.

My life's in the hands of an idiot! Kat warned herself. An older man, immediately to her right, jumped to his feet and roared, "Steer into the skid!" The authoritative voice drowned out other instructions being hurled at the driver.

With trembling hands, he steered left-to-right and then right-to-left, finally regaining control of the bus. Shaken and trying desperately to regroup, he tackled the unruly mob. "Sit down and shut up!" he bellowed. "We're not off this mountain yet!" The bus inched a path around storm debris and continued its journey to the valley below.

Kat, relieved to see the driver was back in command, and the storm losing steam, relaxed her death grip on the armrest. *Maybe I'm not going to die today.*

She turned away from her sister's accusing eyes to watch raindrops splash against the windowpane. She refused to continue defending her choice of transportation. Recently, dealing with Nicole was like trying to navigate a minefield; if you didn't watch your step, the results could be explosive. The death of her two-year-old son was such an unusual and unexpected event; a simple cold spiraled out of control and turned deadly. The consequences of the loss eventually led to emotional estrangement, apathy, and indifference toward her marriage. Ultimately, divorce was the only solution. Kat knew Nicole would never get over the loss of her son, but it was time for her to let go of the grief. No way was she going to give her sister the opportunity to back out on the trip. Nicole needed to move on and rebuild her life.

Nicole said nothing, but she glimpsed something in Kat's eyes just before she turned away, and she didn't like it, not one bit! The look of concern mingled with something else... pity. Angry, she decided to ignore her sister. Listening to the tempo of the wipers, she kicked off her leather flip-flops and settled back into the cushiony seat.

Mariah picked up on the negative vibes coming from the sisters. The sibling squabble sucked every last particle of positive energy out of the air like a black hole attracting light to its darkness. She had learned not to intervene in a conflict between the two. It was a no-win situation for the referee. Staying neutral while identifying the villain and the victim of the conflict never turned out well for her. One of the two always retaliated by turning her ire on Mariah.

Her thoughts were interrupted as she caught a slight whiff of something. It floated on the air briefly and then was gone. She recognized the woody, sweet like aroma of newly crushed tobacco. Her grandfather always kept a tin of pipe tobacco sitting near his rocker. The same tart, deep cherry scent would ease into every room when he smoked.

Is some idiot really smoking? She looked around. None of the passengers had a guilty face. *Strange, smoking on buses and planes had been banned for years.* Giving up on finding the offender, she turned and stared out into the rain-streaked night. There was an ominous feel to the lengthening shadows of the misshapen and twisted trees lining the road.

O-o-oh, Lord! Mariah shuddered in response to a sudden shiver. "Someone just walked over the ground that shall be my grave." She quoted an old wives' tale she had heard as a child, a superstition that foretold the approach of trouble.

Reaching into her jean pocket, she dug for the buckeye. The power of the odd-shaped, brown nut wasn't scientific. Just like a rabbit's foot, horseshoe, or four-leaf clover, the buckeye had its doubters. However, it was oddly comforting to roll the talisman between her fingers.

Chapter 2
Present

Traumatized victims yanked items from overhead baggage compartments. One anxious man, duffel bag held high, made a sad attempt at departing. He squeezed past some with ease but did manage to pop Nicole in the back of the head with his luggage. "Hey, slow down! The storm is over, and I'd like to leave this ride in one piece if you don't mind!"

"Sorry," he threw over his shoulder, continuing on his way. "Excuse me... pardon me..."

"What a jerk!" Nicole mumbled. She allowed people in the front rows to exit before stepping to the aisle. Kat and Mariah followed.

Reaching the sidewalk, Kat said. "This is worse than dealing with sleep-deprived Black Friday shoppers. I'm going to get us checked-in before the madness spreads." Kat plotted a course through the foot traffic, no amateur; she elbowed her way to the entrance to be one of the first to confirm room reservations.

"Catch up with you guys later," Mariah waved and drifted toward the park beside the hotel.

Deserted by her traveling companions, trapped in a stream of nighttime sightseers, Nicole caught the scent of the city. A faint hint of wet concrete and asphalt mingled with a musty trace of freshly turned earth. She looked up and down the street. The town with its well-preserved 1800s style limestone buildings, even at this late hour, was teeming with activity. One-of-a-kind shops and restaurants were still open. She gazed at the horseshoe fog that hung over the Basin Park Hotel apex like a good luck charm. Jostled by a

Ghosts of Perry House

couple engrossed in a map, she dodged her way under arched stone columns to the hotel.

Her slender hand grasped the aged bronze handle and pushed the glass front doors inward. Her stomach flutter in fear as if she were about to step off a high cliff into the unknown darkness below. She couldn't help but shiver as her foot made contact with the black and white hexagon tiles of the entranceway. The air turned frosty and trembled. The lobby drifted in-and-out of focus and was finally replaced with images of people from another time. A foyer crowded with women in bonnets and dresses with sweeping skirts escorted by gentlemen sporting derbies and frock coats waited patiently by stacks of brown leather luggage. It was like a dream, only she was awake.

In front of a made-in-stone fireplace, two ladies sat on armless easy chairs fashioned to provide ample room for their voluminous skirts. They faced a red velvet settee occupied by a gentleman reading his newspaper. A porter, bag in each hand, guided a couple around the sitting area and up the stairs, answering questions as he went.

Before the lobby doors swept shut behind her, Nicole looked over her shoulder. The paved street was no more. In its place, ran a moonlit, muddy road. An old-time piano tune channeled her attention to the saloon and the silhouette of a cowboy staring in her direction. Down the wooden steps, he came. Crossing the road, each stride brought him closer to the hotel and Nicole.

Her thoughts raced in circles, desperate to make sense of what was happening. Had a slip in time occurred at the precise moment she had entered the hotel, thrusting her seemingly, into the past? Or was she experiencing some paranormal event... mysteriously traveling through time by unknown means—for unknown reasons?

Confused and frightened, she squeezed her eyes shut and took several deep calming breaths. Hoping for the best, keeping one eye closed, she slowly opened the other while praying time had righted itself.

Chapter 3
Present

Eager to stretch her legs and release the tension of the harrowing bus experience, Mariah took a deep breath and exhaled. Mother Nature had brought a refreshing hint of honeysuckle and left small puddles on the street and sidewalk. The Basin Spring Park was a natural amphitheater carved into a hill of limestone. Terraced flower beds ringed and colored the rock. It was interesting to note that the back of the hotel, where she was staying, also stood against this wall.

Standing beneath a persimmon tree located between the hotel and the park, Mariah peered upward. Through the leaves and fruit, she could see that it stretched

Ghosts of Perry House

nearly to the top floor of the hotel. From a third-story window, a young girl watched. As Mariah raised her hand to wave, the ghostly figure of a woman yanked the child away and closed the curtain. *The dead live here*, flashed through Mariah's mind.

Mariah was no stranger to this sort of activity. In fact, she had always been able to see, feel, and communicate with "earthbound spirits" as her grandmother, with whom she shared this anomaly, called them. However, her gift remained hidden after telling her mother about the ghost that visited her room nearly every night. "Don't be saying stuff like that; people will think you're mad like your grandmother!" Now older, Mariah still concealed her true nature from the outside world.

An eruption of clapping shifted Mariah's attention to a street performer. A bearded young man in frayed blue jeans was singing the blues. Accompanied by a guitar and harmonica, the trio produced an uplifting mood. His open guitar case was receiving generous tips. She gave a little involuntary shudder; a river of darkness flowed beneath the merriment. Couples holding hands, dog walkers, and tourists reading inscribed plaques were oblivious to the strange vibes being given off by the park.

Near one of the Victorian-style light posts, a sudden movement caught the corner of her eye; she whirled... nothing. Moments later, there it was again, another dark flicker just at the edge of peripheral vision. Mariah's dark-brown eyes were drawn to the bluff and the fleeting but distinctly black human shape floating on the winding track leading to a wooden gazebo. The entity lingered at the scenic rest stop. It wanted something from her, but what?

Mariah was not fond of the black shadow people; sneaky supernatural beings, slithering about outside her direct line of vision. Spooked, but determined to

Ghosts of Perry House

get answers, she reluctantly headed to the wooden steps marking the path.

Before she made it to the stairs, the impatient black vapor rushed forward with inky tendrils stretched toward her! The hair on the back of her neck stood up as it brushed her arm at lightning speed. She followed its streaking form to the center of the park, where she felt a violently rotating column of energy whirling around an overflowing fountain. For a brief moment, the shadow figure, nearly seven-foot-tall with no distinct shape, hovered above the churning invisible force and then was sucked into its spinning center. The meaning of the manifestation wasn't lost on Mariah; the fountain with its healing waters was under the protection of a very powerful entity.

So, where I'm staying and the connecting park both host restless spirits of the past. Her eyes darted to the third-floor window of the hotel and back to the fountain. She regarded all supernatural agents with the greatest suspicion, malicious or completely harmless... only time would tell. Definitely, a vacation downer!

Eagar to put distance between herself and the haunting, Mariah worked her way around the performer and his audience, fumbling for the small vial of homemade essential oil in her purse.

Dabbing it on main pulse points; behind ears, wrists, and over the heart, she waited for the calming effect of the lavender. With it came a back-to-reality check. Kat and Nicole would be settling into their room and wanting a drink at the bar. She checked her phone; no text had been received, thankfully. Mariah needed a little more time to process the peculiar events of the park.

Torn, she debated the wisdom of sharing the mysterious experience with her two friends. Kat, just barely surviving the first year as a high school science teacher, was very scientific and a diehard

Ghosts of Perry House

skeptic of anything that slightly smacked of paranormal. Then there was Nicole, still grieving, her mental state was very fragile. Confiding recently, "It's the same each time. I'm awakened late in the night by Zack urgently calling, 'Mamma, Mamma!' In my heart, I know he isn't there, but I can't stop myself. I hurry to his room, hoping this time it will be different, only to find the bed empty."

Leaving the park and crossing Spring Street, Mariah looked back at the hotel. A ghostly white apparition resembling a man in a cowboy hat now rested in the window where she had seen the little girl. She moaned under her breath while fumbling in her front pocket for the buckeye, "Why me? Why now? I'm on vacation. I need a break from all this supernatural stuff!" That was the whole reason for coming to Eureka Springs... healing water... rejuvenating mind, body, and spirit. Even though she didn't want to see, hear, smell, or talk to the ghosts that prowled the park or waited for her at the hotel, it appeared she didn't have a choice. They had reached out; ignoring them was not an option. They had the power to make her much-needed holiday retreat miserable. Contemplating the problem on the yellow lamp-lit sidewalk, she turned and entered Mystic Crystals Boutique.

Releasing the curtain, the cowboy turned away from the window and stepped to the center of the room. He existed in a shadowy world. Escape impossible; all he had left... dark memories.

Chapter 4
Kansas Prairie–1856

Ma was churning butter on the front porch and eight-years-old, Tanner could hear the soft scraping of the wooden handle passing up-and-down, up-and-down, turning the sweet cream into butter as he helped his pa mend the corral. The thought of wild honey and butter on a hot biscuit made his mouth water. Although he hated milking Beauty, their one and only Jersey cow morning and night, he had to admit that it had its rewards. Milk at every meal, rich cream on wild strawberries, and hand-cranked ice cream in the winter when he'd gather enough icicles for his mother to perform this miraculous feat. Summer's mid-morning Kansas breeze was already hot, reminding him that his winter's dessert would be a long time coming.

Sweating and cursing the heat with each thud of the hammer, Pa worked. Tanner revered his Pa's strength and unwavering determination to complete any job he started. Young Tanner was his pa's right-hand man, fetching and helping him with anything and everything. Repairing the coral was the first of many projects Pa had planned. Satisfied with the day's work, Pa celebrated by taking him skinny-dipping in the creek. "We work hard son, but we must play too!"

Ma had surprised them with a scrumptious supper that evening. She had killed and plucked one of her twenty or so chickens and had it fried and heaped up on a big platter in the center of the kitchen table. Vine-ripened tomatoes, skillet-fried taters, and a wild gooseberry cobbler topped off the end of this glorious day.

Tanner was the first to spot dust rising on the eastern horizon. Horses, moving

Ghosts of Perry House

swiftly spelled trouble. His pa said the country was being terrorized by whiskey-drinking, foul-mouthed marauders who were trying to bring slavery into the territory. They burned out and often killed any who opposed them.

Tanner pointed and shouted, "Pa, riders!"

Pa, seeing the dust clouds pushed back his chair from the supper table and took to the front porch with Ma and Tanner close behind. He wondered aloud, "How many riders does it take to raise a storm like that one?" He guessed at least a dozen horsemen were bearing down on them.

He yelled, "Sarah, get inside and bolt the door!"

The riders were getting close—Pa could hear the hoof beats now—probably within minutes of his family. He grabbed Tanner by the shoulders, "Son, run... run for the fields. Hide and don't come out 'til I call for you!"

"No, Pa, please let me help!" Tanner pleaded.

"Hush! Hide and be very quiet."

Tanner escaped to the nearby stand of corn behind the cabin. From his hiding place, Tanner watched as his pa dashed for the rifle propped by the front door. It was too late; two of the six riders had slid from their saddles and trapped him at the bottom of the porch steps. Arms pinned behind his back, he cursed and struggled, but he could not break free. As they pushed him to his knees, two other men kicked open the cabin door. They dragged his ma screaming and kicking down the wooden steps. The skinny man with a pock-scared face forced her to kneel beside his pa.

What he witnessed next, was forever seared into his mind. One man remained on his horse and coldly stared down on his beloved parents struggling in the dirt. "You were warned. It didn't have to come to this," he yelled, pulling his revolver.

Ghosts of Perry House

Tanner's ma was shot first. As his pa cried out, "No!" a second blast rang out. It was over in an instant.

Pointing to the cabin, the executioner ordered a shorter heavy-set man with a red bushy beard, "Dutch, burn'er to the ground!"

The boss man never moved from his saddle as his raiders pilfered the cabin for valuables. Before riding away, they set fire to the homestead and then left in a cloud of dust, just as they had arrived.

Tanner staggered from the field to his parents; he wrapped his arms around the still-warm bodies and wept. Through his tears, he spied the silver watch chain clutched in his father's hand. Reaching out, he gave it a yank, pulling the timepiece from the lifeless fingers. Tanner picked up the watch. It felt good in his hand. He remembered standing with his pa a long time on the sidewalk, looking at the silver pocket watch in the store window. He'd stood in the same place many times before watching his father looking and wishing. But on this day, Pa went inside and asked the clerk to see the watch up close. It would cost him a year of scrimping and saving, but he wanted that watch. He'd been saving as he could for some time. The next week he went back and bought it. For a man of his circumstance, it was an extravagance, but he was glad he had bought it. And now, so was Tanner.

Alone, he sat until dark. The raging fire reduced his home to a pile of smoldering embers. Everything he loved was gone. But now, there was a new fire stirring within him; one that would shape his destiny.

Chapter 5
Present

There was an annoying note in the repetition of her name, "Nicole... Nicole!" Kat's impatient call startled her into opening both eyes. With a quick glance around the hotel lobby, she thanked her lucky stars. Her glimpse into the past had only been a glitch in time... some sort of déjà-vu madness.

Kat, waiting for the elevator, rolled her eyes in exaggeration expressing her irritation. She mouthed, "Hurry up!" while urgently waving for Nicole to join her.

Nicole hesitated, nervous about using the elevator. Something about it made her feel uneasy. Maybe it was the door, opening slowly with an odd metallic screech to let her sister and the other passengers load. Or, maybe it was the dim, flickering fluorescent light in the ceiling. Or, maybe it was the sign pinned to the back of the elevator that read, "Caution: Elevator Capacity—5 people maximum or 1100 pounds. If you violate these guidelines (1) the elevator will stop moving, (2) you will have to wait to be rescued, and (3) you will have to take the stairs." Whatever it was, Nicole held back.

Kat yelled directions, "Third floor!" just before the door shut with a loud clang.

Nicole decided not to wait for the elevator and headed for the stairs; they were safer. In her opinion, elevators were nightmares. She had an irrational dread of being trapped in one for hours by herself. Claustrophobic as a result of an experience in her childhood, being locked in a closet for hours as a Halloween prank by her sister. She now avoided small, confined spaces if possible.

Nicole weaved in-and-out of the lobby

Ghosts of Perry House

traffic to arrive at the base of the carpeted staircase. Giving access to all the floors, the narrow steps swept upwards. She ran her hand along the smooth slightly rounded banister as she climbed. Reaching the first-floor landing, she found several couples waiting to enter the Balcony Bar and Restaurant. She walked in front of the elevator and up the next flight of stairs.

On the second floor, she noticed a day spa shared the floor with several guest rooms. Walking around the group waiting for the elevator, she peered up the next set of stairs. She took the first step, then another, and another. It felt unnaturally still; the only sounds she could hear were her own breathing and the soft creaking beneath her feet.

She paused halfway up. Something wasn't right. The silence had become oppressive and the air heavy as if before a storm, almost suffocating. She took a shaky step; heart beating faster and faster as she gripped the handrail with white knuckles. She couldn't shake the feeling she was being watched. Nicole quickly looked over her shoulder down the way she had come... nothing. She wiped a bead of sweat from her forehead with a quivering hand and took yet another step. The old staircase moaned with every slow footfall. Determine not to let her fears overcome reason, Nicole gave herself a mental shake. She warned, *Stop letting your imagination rule your emotions!* She took a deep calming breath as she reached the final step and the third floor.

The first thing she noticed was the "Arts and Craft" style decor. Chair rail molding divided the wall. The lower half was covered with Victorian-style wallpaper, a bold print of flowers and foliage in shades of green. The upper half was painted a rich, dark green to complement the paper.

Framed photographs hung high on the walls all along the dimly lit hallway.

Ghosts of Perry House

Intrigued, she started with the one nearest the elevator. Closely examining the details, Nicole went from picture-to-picture. She discovered each black and white photograph told a part of a story that was the early history of Eureka Springs, reminders of the way things used to be. Pictures of wooden buildings, dirt streets, horse-drawn wagons, women in Victorian dresses with flowing skirts, and men on horseback; links to those who were no longer with us.

Near the end of the hall, she stopped. Something about the three-story, white wooden structure in the photograph caught her attention. Stepping closer, she noticed a horse tied to the railing in front of the building. The caption read, "The Perry House 1890."

A shadow flickered at the corner of her vision, startling her. Whirling around, Nicole saw nothing but the empty hallway and the faces in the portraits staring down at her. She swallowed nervously and walked back to the elevator. She couldn't help but feel she was not alone. As she stood there, she caught a scent lingering in the air: acrid, sharp. Not quite burning leaves, but similar. *Tobacco smoke?* she quietly questioned. *Odd, this is a smoke-free hotel.*

Checking the shadowed hallway again, she froze. A shiver raced down her spine and the blood chilled in her veins. Where an instant before there was no one at all, now stood a tall cowboy, wearing a white canvas duster. She recognized him as the man she had seen crossing the street in her déjà-vu moment in the lobby. Staring at her from under wide-brimmed Stetson, he walked with confidence toward her. As long strides brought him closer, he flashed a crooked smile.

Frantic, wild with fear, she froze. *What should I do... run... scream... call for help?* In the end, she did nothing. The silence pressed in on her. All she could hear was the beating of her own heart and the jingling of spurs as each step brought him nearer. Unable to speak, she pressed her back against the wall and waited.

As he strode past, the cowboy nodded and tipped his hat with a polite, "Ma'am."

Nicole turned. Within seconds, the image of the man began to fade to a shadowy outline then vanished completely. *What in the world is happening?* Nicole wondered. Had this ghost of a cowboy entered her world or was she in his? Either way, the incidents filled her with terror. Her legs felt like they were no longer hers, and she began to tremble.

Chapter 6
Chisholm Trail-1870

Tanner rode into camp greeted by Sam, a young wrangler practicing his roping skills. He climbed down, his legs stiff, his face weary, and handed the reins to the lad as he loosened the girth to remove the saddle from his trustworthy quarter horse. Tanner hoisted the saddle over his shoulder and sauntered toward the chuckwagon as Sam tied his mare to the rope line and tended to her needs.

Hired on as part of a 12-man crew, Tanner's job was to help drive two thousand longhorns hundreds of miles over the Chisholm Trail from the south Texas grazing land north to the railhead in Abilene, Kansas. This undertaking had not been without perils. On the long trip—nearly two months—the cattlemen had forged two major rivers: the Arkansas River and the Red River. They had endured the badlands, climbed mountains, and crossed Indian Territory. They had faced down rustles and fought the weather. And they had done all of this while trying to corral a herd of contrary longhorns.

Slapping his goatskin gloves against leather chaps, Tanner headed for the campfire where three cowhands were silently sipping coffee. *It didn't matter how rough men were,* Tanner thought, *let death visit camp, and it puts them to thinking.*

He dropped his saddle near the men and walked to the back of the chuckwagon. He relived the hell of the stampede as he rinsed hands and face from the small pan of water.

It had all started around midnight. The wind picked up, howling over the bare Kansas prairie stirring up dust. With a soft creak of old leather, Tanner shifted his frame in the saddle, tugged the brim of his hat lower over his eyes, and pulled the bandana up over mouth and nose. As usual, the animals were jumpy and skittish before a storm. They would not bed and were restlessly moving here and there.

Back at camp, the cowpokes watched the skies. Soon the full moon was obscured by dark-grey rain clouds. "Come on, boys," the old hand said to the younger men gathered around the cook fire. He knew what was coming. He saddled up and took out across the plains toward the herd followed by every man in camp.

Then it hit in a full fury of wind and rain. A sudden golden streak of lightning ripped open the heavens. Cattle bellowed in fear. A second bolt illuminated the plains—the terrified cattle and the riders stood out in the eerie bluish moment—and then all hell broke loose.

A rider's horse reared and shrieked

Ghosts of Perry House

with terror, throwing the man. Tanner heard the fear in the man's voice as he yelled, "Tanner, over here!"

A vengeful grin spread behind Tanner's bandanna as horns clashed, hooves pounded, and the ground shook. With a roar like an earthquake, the herd ran trampling the downed man, drowning out the screams.

Tanner could have saved the horseless rider, but he didn't. He had recognized the cowhand the day he signed on for the cattle drive. The squinty eyes and pockmarked face was the same that looked down cruelly on his mother while she was shot that day by the big man on horseback.

The man deserved no mercy for the wrong he had done, Tanner thought, turning his attention to the stampeding cattle. He knew holding the herd was out of the question. The only thing to do was for someone to get in the lead alongside the longhorns and try to head them running in a circle before they scattered to hell and gone.

Tanner couldn't see the herd or the other riders except when a flash of lightning lit up the sky. He rode at a dead run in the dark down the retreating column to get up beside the leaders at the head of the stampede. Joined by another rider, they were able to turn the steers to the right forming a circle. The other men posted their locations by firing several shots at a time while keeping the herd rushing wildly round and round. They worked at tightening the circle until the cattle ran themselves out.

Several cowboys began singing to the exhausted animals. The lullaby soothed the jittery longhorns. The herd, well over its scare, was returned to their bed-ground near camp.

Cooke interrupted Tanner's thoughts. "Bacon in the pan, coffee in the pot," he said, pointing to the fire. He then filled a tin plate with beans, lifted the Dutch oven lid

Ghosts of Perry House

and scooped out a hot biscuit, and handed it to Tanner.

Tanner helped himself to several slabs of meat, poured a cup of strong black coffee, and squatted with the others.

A wrangler known only as Cactus Jack said, "The way I figure it, the pace we're settin' ought to have us in Abilene by tomorrow. I don't reckon the boss would begrudge us seein' the sights." All eyes turned on Cactus Jack in surprise. That was as many words as he had spoken since they had left Texas.

"I hear it's a wide-open town." Cooke smiled and added, "Gambling, whiskey, and fancy women!"

"How 'bout good eats?" Billy, the youngest of the men, teased Cookie.

The men continued laughing and joking about the good times to be had in Abilene. Tanner didn't join in. Stomach full, he stretched out on his blanket and watched the darkening sky. The coyotes tuned up for their evening concert, and somewhere in the distance, a cow bawled for her lost calf. He felt the flames of vengeance licking at his soul. No matter how long it took, he vowed to hunt down the rest of the men who had murdered his parents. He whispered to the night, "I will kill 'em all."

He had learned to rope, ride, and use a gun in Kansas on the farm of the family who took him in after the murdering thieves had destroyed his family and burned his homestead. The farmer and his wife were good people, but as soon as he was able to take care of himself, he left and finally wound up in Texas on the JA Cattle Ranch. Owned by John George Adair and Charles Goodnight, the ranch encompassed some million acres of land and a herd of 100,000 cattle.

On the trail, life was rough and monotonous. He was in the saddle for fourteen to sixteen hours during the day and several additional hours during his night shift. Between night duty and early rising, he could never get more than a few hours of sleep. It was dirty, smelly, dangerous, and exhausting work for only $25 a month. He had faced storms, stampedes, rattlesnakes, Indians, and outlaws. He decided, *No more driving longhorns and eatn' dust. Abilene is end of the trail!* Besides, the way he figured it, if Abilene was a "wide-open" cow town as Cooke had said, the big man and the rest of his band would ride in sooner... or later, and he would be waiting.

Chapter 7
Abilene, Kansas-1871

"**We'll** be travel'n 'bout daylight. If you're not here, we'll leave without ya." The trail bosses' words came back to Tanner as he walked down Texas Street away from the Drovers Cottage Hotel and the Great Western Stockyards.

When the herd was sold, he drew his pay. He purchased a completely new change of clothes, from tight-fitting dress boots to a new Stetson. He removed the grime of the trail, visited a barbershop, then donned his new duds and strapped on the pearl-handled Colt. He had no intention of returning to Texas. He had business in this railroad cow town.

Drovers Cottage, a three-story wood-

Ghosts of Perry House

frame structure with about a hundred rooms, had been his home for the rest of the summer and the winter. The broad veranda along the front of the hotel afforded him a perfect vantage point of the town and stockyards. Tenants included mostly drovers and cowboys, but there was a third group calling the hotel home. They divulged very little about their past, and nobody ventured to press the point. Tanner fell into this last group.

He liked Abilene. Wild and untamed, it was like no other. Half the year, it was like most of the sleepy frontier towns across Kansas. But with spring, Abilene quickly transformed into a violent and dangerous boomtown. Thousands of longhorns from Texas began to arrive, and the streets teamed with rowdy drunken cowboys.

Tanner was betting it was a place the men he sought would be drawn to; a town drowning in greed and easy money. Stores, saloons, and gambling houses competed for the patronage of the cowboys while the dance halls and brothel houses catered to their lusts. A town where good was outmatched by evil.

He turned on Cedar Street, and to all who might take notice, he was just a cowboy out looking for a good time. He appeared to glance with little interest in the Alamo Saloon as he passed, yet his steel-gray eyes missed nothing. It offered a shiny mahogany bar with carefully polished brass fixtures. From the back of the bar, a large mirror reflected the glass bottles of amber liquor. He counted a dozen customers. They looked like bankers and businessmen for the most part, not the kind of people eager to strike up a conversation with a cowboy. *A bit fancy for my taste*, he thought.

It was hard to miss the striking appearance of the man in expensive and showy attire playing cards at one of the gaming tables that covered the entire floor space. Yellow wavy hair down to his shoulders, piercing gray eyes, and flowing

Ghosts of Perry House

mustache made Wild Bill Hickok a figure to attract attention. *A good place to stay away from*, Tanner noted.

Hickok, the newly appointed marshal, was well known before he came to Abilene. The deadly marksmanship he displayed in keeping the town quiet and orderly added to his fame. Citizens, drunken trail hands, and Tanner all gave him a wide berth. It was not a good idea to draw the curiosity of this lawman.

Tanner walked on deciding to hunt for a friendlier place. He found it farther down on Cedar Street at the Bull Head Saloon. It was a plain-looking joint with a simple bar of pine lumber for standing drinkers. The main room of the first floor was open to the second story. Half a dozen wooden tables were scattered around, along with chairs. There was a piano to one side of the room although the Bull Head didn't currently employ a piano player. Instead of a mirror, it featured a painting of a woman lounging on a bed with nothing to hide her ample charms except for the strategically placed wisp of cloth. It was the kind of art he could appreciate. He gave it careful consideration while sipping at his drink. The whiskey was passable, and he liked the feel of the place: the lazy undercurrent of trouble that hummed just below the surface of things.

He liked the saloon. He liked the manly smell of beer and tobacco smoke. He liked the easy smiles and flirting manner of the whores. When inclined, he went upstairs to a room with one. He lingered at the bar waiting and watching for the men, five in all, who had ridden into town at sundown. *They'll all be dead before sunrise*, he vowed.

He didn't have long to wait. Out front, riders dismount. Tethering the horses, they tromped, spurs jingling, up onto the wooden boardwalk. Tanner turned in time to see the first through the door, a mountain of a man. Despite the heat, he still wore a long coat, every part of him,

Ghosts of Perry House

from the top of his hat to the worn boots on his feet, was covered in a fine layer of yellowish-brown dust. Tanner noticed the showy way he pushed the side of his coat back, so it caught behind his gun and holster. Four dirt-caked men crowded in behind ready to wash down trail dust and kick up their boot heels. A heavy-set man with red bushy beard was the last to step through the batwing doors.

Tanner immediately recognized the men. Their faces were seared into his mind. They were the other Kansas marauders who had murdered his parents.

"Where can a man get a drink around here?" the big man boomed, suddenly jovial. He strutted to the bar and stationed himself to the right of Tanner. His men followed, lining up along the bar between Tanner and their leader.

The man standing to the left of Tanner gulped his drink, took a lingering look at the painting, and said before scurrying for the street, "You'd better get. That big man is Morgan... John Morgan. He's been causen' trouble in these here parts for quite a spell. Heard he sometimes rides with the Bald Knobbers, vigilantes terrorizing folks in the Ozarks. He's got a streak of mean in him a mile wide. He's apt to kill ya."

Tanner did not acknowledge the warning. Instead, he pulled the silver watch from his vest pocket and flipped the cover. The only thing he had left of his father's, he glanced at the timepiece, and whispered, "Midnight... the killing hour."

Anger contorted his face. He swung around facing the men. "Been lookn' for you boys." he ground out as his right-hand shot down for his gun. The weight of it felt good in his palm as he pulled the iron. His quick-draw was lightning-fast and deadly accurate, lethal retribution for the murder of his parents.

He aimed a shot at the first outlaw in line at the bar and fired. Not having time to turn and draw, the load entered the man's

Ghosts of Perry House

back, tore through his body, and penetrated his heart. He fell face down on the bar blood staining the wooden planks.

Without hesitating and before anyone could react to the attack, Tanner took aim at the next man in the line; the bullet blasted the back of his head. The shot passed through his skull, punctured the brain, and exited below his chin. He crumpled to the floor at the feet of John Morgan and died instantly.

The bar erupted in chaos at the loud explosions and the unexpected smacking sound of bullets hitting flesh. Amidst frightened screams and a stream of cursing, the whores and patrons all scattered. They wanted no part of the quarrel.

"Get that son-of-a-bitch!" Morgan ordered his two remaining henchman. Jerking pistol from holster; Morgan volleyed four shots at Tanner while taking cover behind the bar. The bullets whizzed by Tanner, missing his head as he dove for the floor and rolled behind the nearest overturned table.

The third man at the bar dropped to his knee and fired on Tanner but missed. Tanner returned fire. The bullet struck the gunman in the chest. The wounded man tumbled backward, firing his revolver three times into the smoke-filled room. His bullets pumped into the lifeless back of the first outlaw whose body rested across the bar.

"Bam, bam, bam!" resounded as Tanner returned fired in rapid succession shattering glass and splintering wood. Backing from the blood-splattered saloon, walls riddled with bullet holes, and three dead men, he disappeared into the night. Marshal Hickok would be arriving soon.

The fight in the saloon had lasted but a couple of minutes. The two remaining gunmen had just been warned; they were hunted men.

Chapter 8
Present

"Crap!" Kat swore under her breath. "What the hell is wrong with Nicole, now?" She hadn't even made an effort to catch the lift. Kat stood in the back-right corner of the elevator, contemplating Nicole's behavior. Lately, she had been acting stranger than usual. Kat noticed Nicole would often stare into space with an absentminded smile lost in thought. She complained about being foggy-brained and unable to concentrate. So distracted, she often forgot appointments, where she parked her car, or why she went into a room. Most alarming were the nightmares and sleepwalking. *Were these behaviors normal during grief or was there some-*

thing else going on in that head of hers? Kat worried.

Packed, the elevator groaned from the weight of its seven passengers. There was an elderly couple to her left and two younger couples in front of them. Kat realized that everyone was from the tour bus. The cramped space was hot and uncomfortable, but expecting the ride to be short, it didn't bother her.

The tourists stood patiently. The man to Kat's left was looking at a lobby brochure about a unique underground tunnel tour and stories of Eureka Springs' "Wild West" period. A dull ping announced the first stop.

"Excuse us. This is our floor," said the two seniors. Their exit was abruptly halted by the erratic opening and closing of the sliding doors, snapping like hungry jaws.

"Heaven help us!" the older woman screeched clutching her husband's arm. "Why is this happening, George?" she asked, her voice quivering.

Ghosts of Perry House

"Now Margret, don't let your imagination run away with you," he encouraged, gently patting her hand.

"Did someone push the close button?" Kat demanded.

"No, it seems to be operating on its own!" announced the man in front of the control panel. "Just let me punch some of these other buttons, maybe we'll get lucky," he continued, which got an uneasy chuckle from the rest of the travelers.

Within a few seconds, the smudged chrome jaws halted their reign of terror, and the silver-haired twosome scurried off. The doors begrudgingly closed with a defiant screech.

"Maybe we should've walked the stairs. After that bus ride, I want nothing to do with another near-death experience," proclaimed a lady in front.

"Don't be silly, Honey. Look, we've made it to the second floor! We get off here," her man coaxed, pointing to the indicator light.

Four boisterous young men were waiting to catch a ride as the doors opened. The newcomers stood aside while the husband and his wife departed. The new arrivals were having a conversation about Eureka's week-long Diversity Festival when the elevator lurched and ground to a halt mid-floor.

"We're stuck," one of them announced the obvious.

"Yah, genius!" boomed his taller friend.

Another chimed in with a chuckle, "Looks like a job for the hotel's rescue squad!"

Not amused, the man in the back growled, "If you four idiots hadn't piled on, we wouldn't be in this predicament in the first place!"

The tallest and largest of the young men whirled on his accuser, "Hey man, you talking to me?" Facing each other, the males "squared-off" by flexing their muscles. Next, each drew to his full height and sized up his opponent with puffed chests trying to judge who would win if the verbal back-and-forth came to blows.

Disgusted with the alpha male pissing contest and hoping to defuse the quickly escalating situation. Kat offered, "How 'bout we all just take a deep breath and chill out? This is an old hotel with outdated equipment. I'm sure it's just a momentary mechanical screw-up."

Kat, like millions of others, took elevators every day without giving it much thought. A quick lift usually lasted less than 30 seconds; they were as common and forgettable as yawns, except, of course, until the ride takes an unplanned detour through hell. Now, trapped between floors in a tiny, claustrophobic room suspended by cables in a large, open shaft with openly hostile strangers, she was ready to re-evaluate travel in a five-foot square box.

Just when she thought things couldn't possibly get any worse, the unimaginable happened. The lights flickered for a few seconds then total darkness. It robbed the occupants of their senses and replaced it with paralyzing anxiety.

It was as if she was a passenger on an elevator that had ascended into her very own TV episode of *The Twilight Zone*. At this point in the show, the narrator, Rod Serling, would say, *"You are a voyageur on a crowded elevator... about to embark on a strange journey into the unknown... no return ticket required."*

Kat, boxed in the corner, couldn't move. The human cargo pressed up against her. Someone had been drinking beer and eating garlic bread; she felt like she couldn't breathe. She silently warned herself, *Don't panic!*

One man dug out his cell phone and swung the blue beam out into the darkness illuminating the faces of the victims of the electrical failure. Some put up their hands to shield their eyes, while others squinted and turned away.

The anxiety level in the confined

space spiked. Someone banged on the wall and yelled. A few occupants started to voice what everyone else was thinking.

"What if we're trapped here for the rest of the night?"

"What about water?"

"More important, what about a bathroom?"

One thing Kat had learned in her first year of teaching was that her job was all about crowd control. Teenagers will test teachers, and she had learned two vital strategies when faced with total and utter craziness: 1) take charge and 2) stay calm and don't raise your voice or the situation will rapidly descend into chaos and pandemonium. With this in mind, Kat said, "Sir, shine the light at the control panel." She pushed her way forward and ran a finger down the rows finally stopping on the red emergency button. She pushed. Nothing! She pushed again to no avail.

"Damn it!" Kate ground out between clenched teeth. She prayed, *Please, don't let me be trapped in these cramped quarters with these clowns all night without an adult beverage!* Not giving into defeat, she vigorously pounded the red button until the elevator shuddered and started moving again. Everyone breathed a collective sigh of relief.

"Yah-o-o-o, way-to-go!"

"Hey, thanks, Lady."

On the move, once again, the cabin jerked and began its creaky ascent. Lights blinked off and on and then fully lit up the interior. Cheers sounded from the sardine-packed group as they managed to stay upright. With a jarring jolt the lift arrived at the third floor, the sliding barrier quietly and smoothly glided opened. On wobbly legs, Kat gratefully exited. Glad to find Nicole waiting for her, she grabbed an arm and urged her down the hall to Room 310.

Leaning close to her sister, she whispered, "Whatever you do, **don't** use the elevator!"

Chapter 9
Present

Mariah raised her hand from the oversized treasure chest and immediately knew she was holding something special. The warm feel of it against her skin was oddly comforting. The sand she'd picked up slowly slipped between her fingers, filtering out until all that was left in her cupped palm was a small raindrop-shaped dark stone. It felt like it was vibrating even though it didn't actually appear to be moving when she looked at it.

"Stones speak to each person in a different way."

Looking up in surprise, Mariah noticed the woman behind the counter.

"It's yours. Take it," she continued with

a welcoming smile. "Everyone who enters Mystic Crystals gets a chance at mining for a gemstone. Whatever the customer pulls out is theirs, a complimentary gift from the owner."

Mariah quickly glanced around the shop. She marveled at the brilliance of the crystals and gemstones artfully arranged in glass display cases and on tabletops.

Turning her attention back to the clerk, she held out her prize. "What is it?"

"Apache Tear," the woman responded. "A type of black volcanic rock called obsidian found in the southwestern United States and Mexico."

"Hum... Apache Tear... unusual name for a rock," Mariah commented. Curiosity aroused, she rolled the stone over and over closely examining her treasure.

"Well, it comes from a Native American legend," the shopkeeper began her tale. "It is said that certain members of the Apache tribe were pursued by the U.S. Cavalry to the Sierra Madre Mountains, and although

Ghosts of Perry House

they fought bravely, they were outnumbered. Rather than be captured, they jumped off a cliff to their deaths. The distraught women of the tribe cried dark tears of grief, which fell to the earth and formed into the dark teardrop-shaped stones."

Mariah raised her eyes and met the watchful gaze of the storyteller.

Lowering her voice, the woman continued, "I saw you coming from the direction of the park. It was clear from the look on your face; you had experienced something... something unusual over there. The Apache Tear is a powerful stone. It's your best protection against... whatever is waiting for you," she warned, pointing across the street to the Basin Park Hotel.

Fugitively looking around, as if afraid of being overheard, she explained softly, "Many believe the earthbound spirits of the hotel resisted crossing over into the Light." Moving closer, lowering her voice to a whisper, she finished, "Fearing judgment for their 'sins,' they cling to this earthly realm, reliving the past over and over again."

Chapter 10
Springfield, Missouri-1875

Around noon, Tanner appeared on the southeast comer of Springfield's public square. He spied Dutch on the opposite corner strutting around showing off his late-night poker winnings, Tanner's prized pocket watch.

"I warned you!" Tanner's voice carried across the distance to Dutch.

Dutch, spotting Tanner, laughed and flipped the silver lid on the timepiece, making a big show of checking the hour. The gesture enraged Tanner.

The night before, Tanner, Dutch, and several tinhorns were gambling in the Lyon Hotel, which was located one block south of the square on South Street.

Tanner had been hunting the red-bearded man since the run-in with John Morgan at the Bull Head Saloon in Abilene. It was his good fortune the outlaw hadn't recognized him as the gunman who killed three of his partners that night. The gunplay was over with before anyone could get a good look at the gunman. Tanner, not wanting to push his luck had left town that night. Now, he sat across the green felt table, planning how to kill the man.

Tanner was a good poker player. He prided himself on begin able to outsmart the other players, but not on this night. "Lady Luck" was not on his side. Dutch had "cleaned him out." By the end of the game, Tanner owed the man $25. Foolishly, he'd put the watch up as collateral until he could pay off the debt. However, he issued a warning before leaving the table, "Don't be flashing that watch and bragging 'bout taking it from me."

Of course, Dutch being a natural braggart couldn't resist the temptation of boasting about the card game and his winnings. Drawing a sizable crowd to hear the story, hoping to humiliate Tanner further, he detailed the play-by-play action of the night before. Alerted to trouble by an elbow in the ribs, Dutch paused and scoured the area as the crowd headed for cover. It didn't take long to identify the cause. Recognizing the white canvas duster and black Stetson, he sneered and headed for the man.

"Don't cross over," Tanner warned.

Instead of heeding the warning, Dutch continued his course, drawing his revolver and firing.

It was then that Tanner drew the Colt and fired from a distance of seventy-five yards, shooting his opponent "straight through the heart" reported the coroner.

As Tanner bent to scoop the silver watch from the dead man's hand, an eyewitness to the gunfight exclaimed, "That was one hell of a shot, Mister!"

Chapter 11
Present

The bedside lamp of room 310 cast eerie flame-like shadows that crept up the walls and danced across the ceiling. Nicole rocked legs crisscrossed, Indian style, in the center of one of the two beds, dominating the small room.

"I think I just saw…," Nicole paused, searching for the words that would make her sound sane. Competing thoughts came quickly. *Something happened in the hall… I didn't just make up the cowboy, or did I? Was this just my imagination out of control?*

She tried again to describe her encounter in the hall. "I felt very uncomfortable and even a little frightened

Ghosts of Perry House

of being alone on the stairs, and then I met a man in the hallway…," Nicole's voice trailed off.

Alarmed, Kat joined Nicole on the bed. She recognized that look of bleakness. Nicole was slipping back into the black hole of grief. Not wanting to encourage her sister's imagination, she asked, "Are you kidding? I was trapped in that damn elevator with a bunch of crazed tourists. Now that was scary!"

Heavy footsteps, approaching and stopping in front of the room, drew their attention. What appeared to be the shadow of something on the other side moved from the right to the left. With a click of the lock and turn of the doorknob, breathing suspended, the door slowly creaked open.

Kat jumped to her feet ready to fight as the dark silhouette framed in the doorway stepped into the room.

"Elevator's out of order; had to take the stairs," Mariah announced.

"Damn, Mariah! You scared the holy crap out of us!" Kat complained, clutching her heart.

Nicole agreed, "Next time knock... yell out... do something so we know who it is!"

Mariah closed the door and slipped the antique key into her pocket. The door still had actual key locks; it literally had five locks which included an assortment of chains and deadbolts. *Are these to keep intruders out or keep something more sinister in?* she wondered.

"Why, what's going on?" Mariah asked although it was obvious the white-faced welcoming committee was spooked. Chaos erupted. Nicole and Kat vented, talking over each other and gesturing wildly. Mariah firmly put up her right hand and demanded in an unyielding voice, "One at a time!" The pair of mouths snapped shut. Silence followed.

"Well, one thing's for sure," Nicole finally declared, "this hotel is haunted!"

"Oh, really, and why do you think that?"

Mariah questioned, running her hand along the top of the iron-framed beds on her way to the window. "Definitely not a cookie-cutter, modern hotel suite," she commented. Pulling back the curtain, she confirmed her suspicions. The room looked down on the Basin Spring Park. It was the exact window the spirits had appeared while she was exploring the park.

Nicole hesitated then whispered, "Because I encountered a ghost on my way to the room!"

"A what?" Mariah questioned, pretending to be baffled by the answer.

"I need a shot of tequila!" Kat announced, collapsing on the bed next to her sister.

"What did he look like?" Mariah inquired as she opened the closet door and pushed aside the wooden hangers. "In-room safe and iron and board," she announced, concealing her inner turmoil.

"Well, he was tall. Handsome—in a rugged outdoor sort of way. He was one of those men who radiate danger. Cowboy hat, spurs, and six-shooter strapped around his waist; he looked like he stepped into the present from the past," Nicole explained.

"Did he say anything?" Mariah asked as she stuck her head into the bathroom. "Complimentary shampoo, conditioner, soap and body wash, and plenty of clean white towels."

"Are you looking for something?" Kat asked.

Not detecting anything connected with the paranormal: no extreme sorrow, no feeling of being watched, or even chills during her inspection, she answered, "Nothing, in particular, I just like the quaint old-fashioned style and décor of this place; it keeps the history and authenticity of the hotel intact, and it's probably pretty close to the original Eureka Springs."

Stalling, Mariah crossed the room and stood in front of the oversized gold framed mirror. One thing was certain; they all had experienced something unsettling. But what did it mean? She casually finger-combed a wild tangle of curls back in place and then turned and pointed to the large, screened television mounted on the wall opposite the beds. She smiled. "What more could you ask for?"

Blinking incredulously, Kat answered, "A DOUBLE shot of tequila!"

"Nicole, did he say anything?" Mariah repeated her question, ignoring Kat's dramatics.

"Not much, he tipped his hat and said, 'Ma'am'. But it's not what he said, it's ... he disappeared... vanished."

"Disappeared?" Kat shrieked. Questioning her sister's sanity, she silently wondered, *Is she completely nuts?*

Nicole tried to explain, "When he rounded the corner and headed down the stairs, I couldn't hear his spurs jingle anymore; it was like he just evaporated. He was there, and then he wasn't. There's no other way to explain it."

Mariah rubbed the obsidian teardrop at the bottom of her pocket. In an effort to tamp down the hysterical meltdown looming on the horizon, she cautioned, "Hold on, I want you to remember that this place is old, so the floors creak, the doors squeak, and the hallways are somewhat dark, but this all adds to the atmosphere of the historic hotel. She held up a tourist brochure she had picked up in the lobby. "Keep in mind, this hotel is well known for its rich and colorful history." The fact she emphasized "colorful history" was not lost on her roommates who stole quick glances at each other.

"None of those things explain what I saw!" Nicole insisted.

"I think we'll get some answers tonight." Mariah handed them each an orange voucher.

"What's this?" Kat asked.

Mariah confidently replied, "Our passes to the spirit world... tickets to the *Basin Hotel Ghost Tour*."

Chapter 12
Present

"I'll never make it!" Kat exclaimed, voice fading to a whisper. "Go on without me."

"We're not leaving you behind. You can do it," Nicole urged.

Mariah took another approach. She placed a hand in the middle of Kat's back and gave a not-so-gentle shove. "Move it!"

Out of breath, Kat followed by her two coaches, climbed the last set of stairs to join the other guests waiting on the sixth floor. When she was sufficiently recovered to confront her tormentors, she demanded, "Why? Why did you sign us up for this... this…?" Words failing her, Kat gave up, throwing both arms in the air.

"Hotel slogan might be a clue, *Boo at*

the Basin," Mariah teased as the guide and master storyteller ushered the tour-goers into a brightly lit ballroom.

"Aren't you curious about this town... this hotel?" Nicole inquired, disappointed with her sister's attitude.

"Nope!" she stated unapologetically. Spying the sign over the door opposite the ballroom, the corners of her mouth turned up in a wide grin. "The only thing I'm curious about is if the Lucky 7 Rooftop Bar serves a decent frozen margarita," she declared, breaking away from the group.

"Oh, no, you don't! You're not bailing on us," Nicole scolded, grabbing Kat's arm as she tried to squeeze by.

"We'll stop on the first floor at the Balcony Bar and Restaurant for a beer and burger later," Mariah promised. "Now, come on. I want to get a good seat." Leading the way, she found front row chairs just as the tour guide stepped to the podium and introduced himself as Robert Stemmons.

Ghosts of Perry House

Dressed in the 1920s "Era of the Gangster" fashion: dark pinstriped suit complete with a white band, black fedora hat, he began, "Welcome, and thanks for choosing to spend part of your evening exploring the rich history of Eureka Springs and the 1905 Basin Park Hotel. Outlaws, Indians, gangsters, and ghosts are among the cast of colorful characters whose stories will be part of tonight's presentation."

Nicole leaned forward, not wanting to miss a word of what was to come.

The speaker scanned the crowd trying to gauge their response. Satisfied, he continued. "During the 1800s, Eureka Springs became very popular for its supposed *healing waters*." The waters of the springs were believed to cure various crippling conditions and because of this, the little town's population exploded. By 1880, Eureka was the fourth largest city in Arkansas."

"Nothing new here; straight from the

hotel website," with a smirk, Kat whispered behind her hand to Nicole. All she got for her effort was a loud, "Shhh!"

Not missing a beat, Mr. Stemmons said, "In 1905, the Basin Park Hotel opened. Prior to 1905, the location was home to the Perry House, a hotel which burned to the ground in 1890."

Bored, Kat yawned loudly receiving an elbow in the ribs.

Nicole warned, "Don't start it!"

Pretending to be unaware of the drama playing out in the front row, the historian pointed out the unique features of the vast chamber. "The multicolored stain glass windows that surround this entire room, the hardwood floors, and raised stage made a beautiful setting for the many elegant parties held at the hotel during those beginning years."

"The events were *invitation-only* and required formal attire. Orchestras were regularly used for the dances. It has been reported that late at night visitors to this floor hear music and those who are brave enough to peek through the glass doors have witnessed a fancy ball in progress with dancers swirling the floor in a white shimmering glow."

Signaling his assistant, the lights dimmed, and an image of a darkened ballroom was projected on the screen. Slide after slide flicked into view with each click of the hand-held remote. After several moments, he explained, "Pictures taken by tour-goers in this room have revealed interesting paranormal activity... circular light balls known as orbs. These orbs are thought to be spheres of energy from the spiritual realm."

Kat squirmed on the edge of the wooden folding chair. She couldn't sit and listen to this nonsense any longer. "Some people may wish that orbs are spirits, but that doesn't make it so." She was aware of the sharp intake of breath from the crowd, but it didn't keep her from trying to debunking what she considered a myth.

"Scientists have proven that these objects are nothing more than insects, moisture, dust particles, or...," Kat stopped. She could feel the disapproving eyes of everyone in the room boring into her back.

The storyteller acknowledging the cynic who had interpreted. "Although not everyone believes that orbs indicate the energy essences of a ghost, the Basin Park Hotel is home to plenty of strange and unusual events. Guests sometimes report seeing what looks like tiny lights following them up the stairs or in the hallways. Others have spotted larger and smaller shinning discs both inside and outside of the hotel."

Dismissing the nonbeliever, Stemmons invited, "You're welcome to snap away or to take videos with your cell phone. But, if you capture any strange wispy forms, orbs, or if you're lucky, something resembling a ghostly body, please contact me after the tour. I'd like a copy for future presentations."

Kat sat fuming, while the others

Ghosts of Perry House

including Nicole and Mariah took the tour guide upon his invitation. There was no doubt in her mind, one of the paranormal enthusiasts would claim to discover the image of a ghost on their cell before the group exited the room.

It wasn't long before a man standing next to Nicole exclaimed, "Oh, my, look at this!" He passed his cell around to the gathering crowd. By the murmured comments, it was clear everyone was convinced the strange balls of light caught zipping across the room were spirits from beyond the grave.

For the next ten minutes, there was a flurry of activity as one after another cell phone cameras snapped away. When the lights went up indicating it was time for the next phase of the tour, one lucky ghost hunter proudly shared his video: highly energized orbs performing aerial stunts, diving, and swooping in the dark and cavernous space—bright white and perfectly spherical.

CC Brown

"Definitely not dust particles," the smug, amateur photographer declared for the benefit of the skeptic in the room.

Chapter 13
Present

"**Ok**, folks, gather round," Stemmons urged the stragglers while mentally counting heads. Once everyone was accounted for, he began, "The strange... the eerie... the unsolved begins here on the third floor."

"Third floor! That's us," Nicole mouthed her alarm to Mariah close at her side then refocused her attention on the man in the black fedora.

"The Basin has the distinction of being one of America's most haunted hotels and has even been featured in several national magazines," he announced, standing a little taller, with puffed chest. "The owners believe so strongly in its resident ghosts that they offer tours four nights a week for anyone interested in learning more about these earthbound spirits."

"I have a question," Kat broke in. "If ghosts exist, why are we no closer to finding out what they really are?" Scanning the group, she was surprised to be met with blank stares. She tried again, "The evidence is no better today than it was a year ago, a decade ago, or a century ago!"

One guest explained, "Ghost hunting is not about the evidence, if it was, the search would've been abandoned long ago. It's about having fun with friends, telling spooky stories, and the enjoyment of searching around the edges of the unknown."

Out of patience, Kat shot back, "Don't you get it? It's all about the money: T-shirts, books, videos…"

Fed up with the interruptions, one armature investigator asked, "Geeze Lady, what's your problem?"

The woman at his side added, "We

Ghosts of Perry House

may be spinning our wheels, but at least we're enjoying the ride."

Nicole begged, "Kate, please."

"Yes, knock it off!" Mariah insisted, silencing her mouthy friend.

Stemmons, a seasoned performer, didn't let the sideshow distract the group and quickly redirected attention back to his story. "To understand the recent paranormal phenomena experienced by guests, we have to start at the beginning. The first building located on this site was the pet project of Colorado hotelier, Captain Joey Perry. Perry came to Eureka Springs in 1880 with an incurable disease, which was miraculously cured by the spring water! So appreciative, he chose to give back to the area by building the Perry House Hotel."

"Sounds to me like a man who saw a business opportunity and took advantage of it," an elderly gentleman commented, getting a few chuckles.

"And, the venture was very lucrative,"

Stemmons revealed, "until 1980 when a fast-moving fire completely destroyed the structure and most of the town. Fortunately, the Basin Park Hotel opened on the same site several years later. Soon after, guests began to report strange occurrences. Many different paranormal groups have conduct research over the years, and many of those groups picked up voices on recorders and electro-magnetic spikes in the hallways and rooms on this floor."

Walking slowly down the corridor, he pointed to the gold numbers on each door. "The most active rooms are 307... 308... 309 and..." He paused for effect and then ended with, "310." Nicole gasped, "310? That's our room!"

All heads pivoted in her direction. A slight smile turned up the corners of Stemmons' mouth. Revealing the room numbers always got a reaction. Satisfied, he continued, "Stories involving entities on this floor included a man in a cowboy hat

Ghosts of Perry House

known to walk through rooms, into the walls,... vanishing no less."

"I didn't imagine him," Nicole said, taking a step closer to Kate, hoping to not be overheard. "See, I'm not crazy!"

The guide went on to provided details of other reported sightings. "A female spirit is said to visit patrons after midnight. Pale blonde-haired and dark blue eyes, she never seems to bother anyone but clearly isn't happy. Her appearance is in sharp contrast to the little girl also spotted playing in the halls, usually described as between the ages of five and eight with hair pulled back in two pigtails."

Mariah realized the puzzle pieces were all falling into place. Spirits of the dead, trapped between this plane of existence and the next, were desperately trying to make sense of an existence that by definition makes no sense at all. She moved closer to the speaker, listening intently for more clues.

"Sometimes guests on this floor report

detecting the charming aroma of cherry tobacco, both while alone and while on tour with me. The most bizarre event," he explained, "came during a recent tour of twenty-four people. We all simultaneously experienced the unique scent which lingered for well over a minute. And let it be understood that our entire hotel is a *non-smoking* property and has been for years."

That explains the tobacco smell, Nicole thought.

Mariah examined the faces of the tour-goers. It was clear each was eager to see something, feel something, or smell something that they could categorize as a ghostlike experience.

She stiffened. Cold that came from no one place, yet from everywhere crept over her. She realized others were feeling the same numbing chill when the young woman nearest her turned pale and quickly asked, "Did anyone feel that?"

"It's the little girl," a woman from the back spoke up. "She's here. I feel her!"

Ghosts of Perry House

Adding to the hysteria, a man held his phone high and commanded, "Look at this!" On the screen, a shapeless foggy mist hovered directly in front of Mariah.

Narrowing her gaze, Kat made eye contact with the owner and questioned, "Aren't you the lucky one? Two ghost pictures in one night: ballroom and here on the third floor. What are the chances of that?" she asked, a sarcastic grin tugging at the corners of her mouth.

To his credit, the man ignored her barbs and handed the cell to Mariah.

Mariah reviewed the picture displayed on the screen. Tiny pin prickles at the base of her neck warned, "Beware!" She lifted her eyes and slowly searched the shadows of the dimly lit third floor. They were being observed by an unseen presence... *little girl... woman in white... or cowboy with a six-shooter? Which one?* she wondered.

"What do you think?" Mariah asked the guide.

Stemmons responded by placing a small handheld device on the carpet at her feet.

"What are you doing?" she asked, stepping back from the man and his gadget.

"This is an EMF meter," he answered. "It detects electrical emissions given off by spirits of the dead." As if on cue, the meter went crazy beeping and flashing.

Continuing the show, he requested, "If there is indeed a spirit present, please make the meter slow down." Like a curtain, silence fell upon the group; the meter slowed down immediately. After moments of heartbeat-like pulses from the machine, he demanded, "Spirit, speed the meter back up." No one dared move—breathe, and then, the meter ramped up to a fever pitch, rocking violently for a few more moments then went dormant.

"We just witnessed a visit from the afterlife!" an excited spirit tracker declared.

Paranormal derangement syndrome, Kat thought, shaking her head from side to side. EMF meters detect electrical current; every electrician carries one. Obviously, the floor and walls were riddled with wiring. *Don't have to be a science teacher to figure that out.*

"Something like this doesn't happen every night," Stemmons proclaimed, "but sometimes it does. It's this unknown factor and the many documented accounts that have made the ghost tours in our mountaintop spa resort so popular. That is why believers and non-believers," he glanced at Kat and then resumed, "can enjoy and co-exist on our tours. Some come to find proof, some come to debunk, but all come to have fun." He finished, leading the group down the stairs to the final phase of the tour.

Chapter 14
Present

The guided tour descended three flights of stairs to a shadowy cave-like room. The yellow-white glow of hundreds of candles relieved the darkness just enough to reveal metal folding chairs along one limestone wall. When seated, guests were treated to samples of locally distilled whiskey reminiscent of the bootleg liquor once served at the hotel.

"Best part of the tour," Kat muttered, her appreciation for the once illegal refreshment apparent as she accepted the small plastic sample cup with enthusiasm.

Absently sipping the strong amber drink, Nicole's graze was drawn to the beauty of the burning candles. The light

Ghosts of Perry House

from the blackened wicks flickered as wax slowly turned to liquid, running down the sides and onto the rocky ledges below.

Mariah broke the spell. "Candle burning is the simplest form of magic."

Nicole, seated in-between her sister and friend, shook off the trance-like feeling and gently massaged her temples.

Overhearing Mariah's comment, Kat spoke in a low voice, "And, cheap tricks impress gullible ghost hunters."

Sighing, shaking her head, Nicole pleaded, "Please, you two. It's not necessary to share every idiotic thought that pops into your heads!"

Before either woman could respond, Mr. Stemmons cleared his throat signaling he was ready to begin. "From the time of the Wild West to a time marked with illegal liquor and speakeasies, the hotel with its unusual amenities has long provided an ideal sanctuary for a certain clientele. Built into the side of a mountain, every floor at the rear of the six-story building is at ground floor making it perfect for those needing a quick escape."

Listeners turned and craned their heads to get a better view as the speaker gestured toward the back of the room. Two boards crisscrossed a door blackened and chard from where flames had once scorched the wood. "And the catacomb of secret caves and underground tunnels connecting the Basin Park Hotel with other buildings provided a safe space for unwholesome activities including boot-legging during Prohibition."

Anticipating tunnel tour requests, Stemmons was quick to state, "The hotel entrance to the underground is now boarded up for the safety of our guests."

Or, Mariah silently added, *to keep the spirits of the tunnels forever trapped in the maze of dark passageways beneath the town.*

"Interested?" Stemmons inquired then informed the audience, "Tickets for the seventy-five-minute walking tour are available at the Eureka Underground kiosk located in the Basin Spring Park."

Kat perked up. *Catacombs... underground tunnels... secret passages, finally something interesting!* She had recently read an online article about the ancient Catacombs of Rome. Doubtful she would ever make it to the Italian city; she thought a tour of Eureka's underground might be the next best thing.

Putting her hand on Nicole's arm, Kat leaned in and whispered, "Want to investigate the secret passages?"

Making eye contact, Nicole answered, "No way! I'm surprised you even had to ask. Think... claustrophobic... fear of confined places. There's nothing scarier to me than a small dark tunnel."

"Sorry, can't keep track of your psychosomatic disorders," Kat grumbled sarcastically. *Geez, she is never going to forgive me for that Halloween prank!* Kat thought, looking away from her sister's accusing glare.

CC Brown

Sick and tired of her sister's attitude, Nicole pried the fingers from her arm. "You know Kat, some things aren't funny, just mean!" Nicole declared. Hoping she hadn't missed anything important; she redirected her attention to the speaker.

"During prohibition and well into the 1950s the hotel was a haven for those looking to party in style. Restaurant patrons were invited to dine on trout taken from the cold waters that once ran through this cave. After, they could dance the night away at the popular fancy ball on the sixth floor or move on to drinking and playing the slot machines at the Lucky 7 Rooftop Bar."

A man from the audience spoke up. "Beats Moneyland bingo! Didn't win a single game!"

After the laughter died down, the guide spoke directly to the bingo man. "You would have enjoyed the hotel's unique venue then. It quickly gained a reputation for being a fun vacation destination. The rich and famous flocked to this remote Ozark Mountain town and the hotel for the entertainment offered: gambling and liquor by the drink."

Puzzled, the same man asked, "What happened?"

"The town sheriff happened. He descended on the hotel one night in 1955 along with dozens of officers wielding weapons and search warrants. He arrested several people and confiscated all slot machines, ending the hotel's gambling and speakeasy era."

Winding up the session, Stemmons issued an invitation to the guests, "During your stay, listen carefully and you may hear the bells of the slot machines ringing on the sixth floor or the soft sound of a waltz coming from the ballroom. If you're lucky, you may even see the cowboy who still roams silently through the rooms and halls."

Curious, Mariah raised her hand. "Do you believe the hotel is haunted?"

The guide chose his words carefully, "Well,... I admit there is something here. And personally, I've noticed and felt things which couldn't be explained. Many guests over the years have claimed to see strange movement through the darkened halls, having ghostly visits in the middle of the night, and hearing whispers and unexplained noises. My job is to tell the story of the hotel; I leave it to each of you to decide if indeed it's haunted."

Taking off his hat, Stemmons ran one hand through his hair. "I've identified the hot spots, the places with the most paranormal activity. If you're interested in investigating on your own, several guests have reported having fun with a new app called *Ghost Hunting Detector*. This ghost detecting tool claims to translate electronic voice phenomena, undetectable by the human ear, into letters that then form written words from the spirit world. You can download it to your cell phones and check out the hotel on your own!"

This bit of information got an immediate reaction from most of the crowd. Phones clicked on and fingers tapped away on miniature keyboards, accessing the internet in an effort to locate and download the app.

Replacing the fedora, Mr. Stemmons dismissed the group with, "Goodnight and enjoy your stay at the Historic 1905 Basin Park Hotel." He paused and then finished with a warning, "Remember, 12 midnight is known as the 'Witching Hour.' The time when the veil between the realms of the living and the dead is at its thinnest, allowing spirits to travel between the two worlds."

Chapter 15
Present

Drink untouched, Kat studied the small audio recorder placed in front of her. She crossed her arms atop the table and looked up at the owner. Something was off, but she couldn't put her finger on it. She listened to her gut instinct. Like a lioness on the prowl, she stayed alert and watchful.

After the ninety-minute ghost tour, she had followed Mariah and Nicole to the Balcony Bar and Restaurant for a little R and R. Taking a table in the outdoor seating area, she was enjoying the late-night view of downtown Eureka Springs when this guy showed up.

The attractive intruder leaned back against the rail overlooking Spring Street.

He casually glanced at the crowd of tourists below and noted the slow crawl of traffic before directing his attention back to the women.

"What'd you think?" he asked with a disarming smile, revealing perfect teeth and an even more charming personality.

Mariah tilted her head slightly to one side, confused, but working hard to understand what was going on, answered his question with a question, "About what?"

"You know, 'bout the ghosts," he probed.

"What ghosts?" Kat countered, giving nothing away.

With a twinkle in his dark eyes, the man gave her that *you've got to be kidding* look, and then said, "I'm agnostic about ghosts; I've never seen one but can't disprove them, either. I got interested in all this spirit stuff through watching ghost-hunting shows on cable. Decided this spring to invest in a few tools of the trade. And here I am."

I knew it, Kat thought. *An armchair ghost-hunter turned pro. Basic training—hours of big-screen TV with a direct link to crazy!*

She confronted him head-on, "You do realize reality TV ghost-hunting shows are worthless. They do entertainment, not science. It's all about ratings. Dedicated fans, like yourself, continue to tune-in even though not one of these programs has ever captured any evidence of life after death. Still, you watch every week, thinking this time will be different."

The man pulled out the empty chair next to Kat and sat without being invited. He introduced himself. "I'm Steve. I remembered you gals from the tour."

"And I remember you from the bus. You were the guy bludgeoning people with your duffle bag," Nicole pointed out.

"Yeah, sorry about that," he apologized, not letting the less than warm reception stop him. What he had to share was more important than the rules of etiquette. He paused, waited for an introduction, and when it didn't come, continued unphased. "Ladies, it's clear that visitors from beyond the veil are reaching out to us. The only thing we don't know is—why? With the advances in science and technology in the last century, I believe that at some point in the very near future, we'll solve this mystery."

Kat frowned and stared disapprovingly at the intruder. *He thinks we're like him, paranormal chasers.*

Perplexed, she looked across the table at her sister to find questioning sapphire-eyes staring back. Kat didn't like all this talk of things beyond the scope of normal scientific understanding. It was not good for her sister to be exposed to all this radical nonsense. She felt Nicole's recent interest in the supernatural had roots in a desire to regain control over her world after the passing of her son. After all, a world where random bad things happen to good people is far more nightmare-inducing than a historical hotel with a "colorful" past.

"Let me explain," Steve began, interrupting her thoughts. "I'm in room 307. During my stay, I took several hundred infrared photographs around the hotel, used my EMF detector near every reported hot spot, and ran a constant audio recorder in my room. They revealed nothing—until this evening."

Interested in where this was going, Nicole asked, "And…?"

Encouraged, Steve scooted his chair closer and lowered his voice. "While away from my room tonight, grabbing some dinner before the tour, the recorder actually captured a couple of interesting things," he shared, reaching out and punching the play button.

Kat, Nicole, and Mariah leaned forward, oblivious to everything going on around them. Their attention fastened on the small black box. They listened intently, stretching, and straining to hear. A few

Ghosts of Perry House

moments of silence were followed by the creak—creak—creak of wooden floorboards as if someone or something was hurriedly moving about the room.

Steve paused the recording, looked around the table, and then said, "This is especially odd because there is no indication of a door to the room opening or closing prior to or after the captured footsteps."

"Now, listen closely to this next segment," he instructed starting the recorder once again. The barely audible sound, maybe a voice, could be detected before the recorder went silent. With a crooked smile and a wink at Kat, Steve turned off the machine, pushed back his chair, and stood.

He's a charmer alright, Kat thought, but it would take more than a good-looking man with a manipulative personality to change her mind.

Before leaving, Steve added one last thing for the woman at the table to mull over, "Though it's not enough to definitely tell whether the speaker is female or male, it's definitely the voice of someone... or something."

Nicole had no doubt who was speaking, the cowboy. It was clear from his voice something horrible—something unthinkable was happening. A whisper, laced with dread, repeated the same word over and over until the tape went silent.

"What was he saying?" Kat asked, looking around the table.

"Well, sounded like a name... Mort or Morton," Mariah guessed.

"No, I think it was Morgan. Yeah, definitely Morgan," Nicole insisted.

The minute Steve stepped away and rejoined his group, a heated argument immediately ensued between Kat and Nicole.

"Surely, you aren't taken in by this guy's bogus claims. He probably made the recording with his buddies to dupe gullible people just like you," Kat warned.

Arching eyebrows, Nicole replied with a self-satisfied shrug.

Kate exploded, "Geeze, you are so naïve!"

Determined note to be bullied, Nicole stubbornly insisted, "It was the cowboy; I recognized his voice. He was repeating that name. It must mean something."

"That doesn't make any sense." Kat rolled her eyes and looked at Mariah for backup. Not getting any, she proceeded to make her case, "A creaking floor and a barely audible whispered voice does not—let me repeat, does **not** make a haunting!"

"What about the elevator?" Nicole offered.

"Mechanical failure," Kat shot back.

Not willing to give in, Nicole thought for a moment, "Orbs in the ballroom?"

A self-satisfied smile tugged at the corners of Kat's mouth, "Dust particles."

"Ok, explain the wild beeping and flashing of the EMF meter," Nicole insisted.

Kat tapped her foot in noiseless irritation. "Electrical wiring." Tired of Nicole's nonsense, she tried one more time. "There is no concrete evidence of ghosts. Every unexplained occurrence you claim is supernatural has a scientific explanation. Face it, Nicole, no matter how much you want it to be true, ghosts are not real!"

Mariah listened, turning her head from sister to sister as they tried to poke holes in the other's case. Finally, she intervened, "Kat, consider this, hauntings can be subtle. They're not all about an apparition appearing and yelling, 'Hey, I'm here!' Sometimes we have to pay attention to the little thing going on around us."

Feeling she had the strongest argument but realizing she was outnumbered, Kat good-naturedly agreed to a temporary truce. She gave in with a smile, "Ok, let's agree to disagree on matters of the spirit world."

Mariah shook her head in agreement and changed the subject hoping to reduce the tension between the two sisters, "What's the plan for tomorrow?"

Ghosts of Perry House

Nicole, still peeved, answered first, "Souvenir shopping."

Kat, unable to resist one last jab at her irritated sister, announced, "Explore Underground Eureka—alone since Nicole finds small dark places emotionally challenging."

Against her nature to lie, Mariah weighed the pros and cons of being completely honest with her friends, and then said, "It's the historical museum for me. I'm intrigued by this town and its unique history."

Mariah chose to leave out the other reason. In the 1800s the only men who wore a six-shooter strapped to their hips were cowboys, lawmen, or outlaws. So, which was the ghost Nicole was so taken with... law-abiding citizen or stone-cold killer? She suspected hidden deep in the past and buried somewhere within the historical museum was the answer to the haunting of the 1905 Basin Park Hotel.

Chapter 16
Stone County Missouri-1883

After riding south for some time, Tanner had just about given up when he drew upon a ridge that looked down on what he was searching for, Morgan's hideout. "The remoteness probably added to its appeal for the outlaw," Tanner surmised. On his search, he had followed a trail that took him through thick stands of sassafras, cedar, and oak in Stone County, Missouri. It was a maze of steep hills, sharp ridges, and streams with chert-clogged channels. *If you break the law and don't want to get caught, this would be a good place to hide,* Tanner reasoned.

He casually took the sack of tobacco and packet of rolling papers from his vest pocket. Peeling off one of the thin sheets, Tanner rolled a cigarette and lit it. He took a drag. Shaking out the match, he dropped it to the ground.

He studied the weather-beaten shack and dilapidated barn as he enjoyed his cigarette. Smoke waffling from the old crumbling chimney signaling someone was inside. No horses tethered out front at the hitch or loose in the paddock made Tanner think he had missed John Morgan and his band of outlaws. But maybe he could leave a message for the big man... one a ruthless murder like Morgan could understand.

He tossed the butt and slowly rode down the steep hillside to the homestead. As he reached the yard, a young man stepped from the shadows of the barn with a shotgun folded in his crossed arms.

"Who are ya, Mister?"

"I'm a stranger. You don't know me."

"Well, what do ya want?"

"I'm looking for John Morgan."

A worn-looking woman with a pistol at her side stepped to the doorway of the shack, shielding someone behind her. "What do ya want with my husband?" she asked, voice gruff and demanding.

"Well, Ma'am, I intend to kill him," voice cold and stare even colder, Tanner replied politely.

Not liking the answer, the boy and the woman both leveled their guns at Tanner. Tanner reacted to the threat with a quick draw and three shots. The first sent the boy backward, dead before he hit the ground. The second spun the woman around. She crumpled to the floor with a groan. As she fell, Tanner fired his last shot. The light from the fireplace played over the bodies and the pooling blood. The woman was dead, but a small boy lay beside her holding his cheek: bleeding and moaning.

Tanner started to dismount to finish the job but then hesitated. *What satisfaction will come from slaying a child?*

he wondered. Reining his mount, he rode back the way he came. He figured the nearest town was at least a day's ride.

Chapter 17
Ozark Missouri-1889

"**Any** last words?" Sheriff Zacharis Johnson asked the four handcuffed men standing on the scaffold platform. The end of the Civil War had brought dangerous men to southern Missouri and northern Arkansas; men who had cut their teeth on killing. It brought men like John Morgan and vigilante groups like the Bald Knobbers. The sheriff's job was to bring the lawless to justice.

Morgan defiantly stared at spectators jostling to get a better view. Finally coming to the realization, it was the end for him, he spat and cried out, "Get it over with!"

Tanner watched the proceedings with interest. He had arrived in the Christian County town of Ozark shortly after first reading about the Bald Knobbers in the *Kansas City Star*. More than eighty members of the vigilante group including John Morgan were charged with crimes from unlawful assembly to first-degree murder. The group had been terrorizing the hills and hollers of the Ozark Mountains for years. Their distinctive hoods, designed to strike fear in their victims, were made of cloth bags with the top two ends dyed red and tied to look like horns.

Best he could figure from the newspaper account, the Civil War was being reenacted in the Ozarks. The Bald Knobbers were ex-Union soldiers now businessmen. The original group was said to be about a dozen and went by different names, but the one that stuck was the "Bald Knobbers," given because the group met in open, bald space on the top of the area's prominent hills, called "knobs." The other side tended to be ex-Confederates and longtime residents, most farmed for a living. The businessmen looked down on these native "hill men," as backward. Over the years, it was unclear how many died in the fighting between the two groups. The reporter's estimates ranged from a dozen to more than thirty, with countless more beaten and driven from their land.

Governor Marmaduke who, strangely enough, was a former Confederate general, was quoted in the newspaper, "The lynching, night riding, and shootouts must be stamped out. I don't care who fought for which side; I just want the killing to stop."

The governor got what he wanted with the arrest of eighty Bald Knobbers. The newsworthy story of the indictment and trial appeared on the front page of every paper across the nation even the prestigious *New York Times*.

Meanwhile, in Ozark, amid an almost carnival-like setting, the inevitable group of loiterers sought comfortable positions at points of visual vantage on the bench in front of the dry goods store or on the ground under a tree near one of the courthouse's open windows. These men spent hours following the comings and goings at the building. They knew every witness called to testify, every question asked, and every answer given. They prided themselves in accurately retelling every detail to interested listeners, and Tanner was willing to listen.

Tanner sat under the tree next to one of the old-timers, listening intently to his story. "Well, here's how I heard it told," the old man began, settling back against the tree. "Chieftain of the Bald Knobbers, Dave Walker called a meeting for the purpose of destroying a moonshine still operating in Chadwick. Almost all the Knobbers were there, having given the password to the sentry as they entered the naturally barren top of Snapp's Bald. The roaring fire cast an eerie light upon the masked men. There was not a sound except the crackling of the flames and the occasional nicker of horses and mules.

Walker demanded the moonshiner be

stopped. After a hearty agreement from all present, the men checked and loaded their pistoles, rifles, and shotguns and then mounted their rides. Following single file behind their leader, they left the open area of the bald, down the worn narrow trail cut through the oaks to the rough road below. There were a few occasional words but by the time they reached the cabin, they were completely quiet. However, the masked men found no evidence of the still, and Walker called off the raid."

"Yah, and if the raiders had stopped there, they wouldn't be facing the noose now!" added a dark-haired man as he stretched out under the shade tree to hear more of the tale.

In his lazy drawl, the old man continued his story, "After Walker left, some of the younger and rowdier members of the vigilante group decided to go off on their own and pay a visit to William Eden who had often spoken out against the Bald Knobbers. Finding the cabin empty, the men decided to ride on to Eden's father's cabin just down the road.

A light from an old kerosene lamp flickered inside the cabin as the riders approached. Hearing the hoofbeats, old man Eden stepped out onto the porch. He carried a loaded shotgun with him."

'Who is it?' Eden asked the hooded men.

A muffled voice answered, 'We're the Bald Knobbers, law in these here hills.'

'What do you'uns want?' Eden challenged as he raised the shotgun to his shoulder.

'We're going to teach you to keep your big mouth shut, old man!' the same voice called out.

"Fearing the worse, Eden hurried to get back in the house and bolt the door. It did no good. There were too many of them, and the raiders easily busted open the front door and shot old man Eden standing in front of them with his shotgun in hand prepared to defend himself and

CC Brown

his family. Then they shot Charley Green, paying a visit to the cabin along with his wife, as well as their intended target, William Eden also in the cabin."

"One of the more sensible men finally gained control of the rampaging vigilantes before they shot Mrs. Green. He finally got all of the Bald Knobbers out of the cabin and sent for Dave Walker."

A young man, sounding suspiciously like a Knobber sympathizer, spoke up, "I heard, when Walker got to the cabin and saw the damage, he ordered all of the men to go home."

"I reckon you're right, but it was too late for the three dead men." Tanner pointed out plucking a blade of grass, examining it thoughtfully, and then tossing it aside.

"The way I see it," an elderly listener cut in, "Dave Walker's as guilty as sin. He didn't pull the trigger this time, but he's been in on plenty of other killin's in these here parts."

Ghosts of Perry House

Bring his story to an end, the old-timer finished with, "I was sittin' right here the day Sheriff Johnson testified that upon arriving at the Eden cabin; he talked with, Mrs. Green. She told him she could identify William Walker (Dave Walker's son), John Matthews, his nephew Wiley Matthews, and John Morgan, as well as others involved in the massacre. The next morning, the sheriff said he set about arresting the entire group one-by-one, meeting little resistance."

The day the verdict was announced, Tanner stood outside the courthouse with the elderly storyteller and most of the town's people. A cheer went up inside and outside of the courtroom when the judge sentenced the four to hang. The others were given a range of punishment from $50 fines to several years in the state penitentiary.

"All that's left is the execution," the old-timer said to Tanner before turning and walking to his favorite shade tree. Sitting, he settled back, cupped his hands behind his head, and closed his eyes.

A few months later, Tanner stood in the courtyard outside the jail. A throng of thousands, crowded around to get a better view over the fence erected to protect the victims as well as those responsible for carrying out the punishment. He felt nothing... no hate... no regret... just a numbing emptiness.

"Let's get this over with," the sheriff demanded. This was Johnson's first hanging. He had ordered the carpenter to build the scaffold with four nooses and one large trap door so all the men would be hanged with one drop. Wanting to get it over with as soon as possible, he pulled the lever and the men fell. There was a terrible groan from the onlookers. The men, wild with pain, beat and thrashed around. Gurgling and choking, they twisted to-and-fro, striking against each other, legs intertwining as they struggled in the throes of death. For fifteen minutes, the crowd stood in silence. Finally, all signs of life disappeared from the bodies.

So ends John Morgan's reign of terror, Tanner thought. It was fit that Morgan's death was as agonizing and violent as the crimes he had brought on the helpless people of Kansas and Missouri.

Tanner turned and walked to his horse tied to a hitch in front of the dry goods store. He swung up into the saddle, reined the gelding to the west, and made for Dodge City, Kansas.

Chapter 18
Present

Last to brush her teeth, Nicole and Kat already in bed, Mariah hid the Apache Tear under her pillow, before switching off the bedside lamp. Day one of weekend getaway had been... well... interesting. She slid in-between cool, crisp sheets and quickly drifted into a dreamless sleep.

Instead of waking up in the morning to the beep, beep, beep of the alarm, refreshed and ready to tackle the next day of her weekend getaway, she was awakened in the middle of the night. Disoriented, confused, not knowing where she was, Mariah struggled to make sense of what was happening. Shaking off the fog of sleep, two things were immediately clear: she couldn't move, and she wasn't alone.

She sensed a presence hovering in the dark and felt the suffocating weight of utter silence. Who the hell was in her room? Her mind raced with possibilities as a sudden frosty draft chilled the air; a sign from the spirit world to take notice and pay attention! Someone was reaching out to her.

Unable to open her eyes, her hearing became sharper. Desperate, straining for the slightest sound, she waited. At last, Mariah detected the soft whisper of rustling silk at the foot of the bed, followed by the weight of someone sitting down.

Oh, no! Mariah's mind screamed as long slender fingers wrap her left leg near the ankle. Instantly, a tingling swept her entire body as if she had received a slight shock. She tried to pull away from the cold grip and reach for the hidden talisman beneath her head, but she couldn't move, not even her lips to call out for help.

Trapped, helpless, a sense of panic began to well up within Mariah. Fear gripped her body. She fought with all her strength to sit up, move her arms and legs until she reached a state of pure terror. Exhausted, paralyzed, she realized no amount of fighting could break the spell. She ceased to struggle.

Her breathing came in rapid gasps; heart thumping so loudly she was sure whatever was perched next to her could hear the panic. *Stay calm*, she warned, talking herself through regaining control: *breathe in deeply... hold it... breathe out slowly*. She repeated the process over and over until gradually, the rapid heartbeat and erratic breathing returned to some semblance of normal.

Desperate to discover who or what her bed partner was, Mariah worked harder to open her eyes. Heavy eyelids struggled with surrounding muscles. Finally, after what seemed an eternity, she was able to pry open one eye wide enough to see through lashes. For a few seconds, she could make out nothing at all but dark lumps of furniture: massive wardrobe, easy chair, and end table.

Feeling every heartbeat, Mariah hesitantly focused her attention on the foot of the bed. Posed on the edge was a glowing figure—a woman dressed in a white Victorian-style day gown.

The entity slowly raised her head and looked directly at Mariah. Sadness and sorrow filled the dark space between them. Bitter agony, void of any hope or joy, so deep nothing not even eternity, could ease the pain, reached out to Mariah. Her throat tightened in unshed tears of compassion.

She wondered how any being—living or dead—could long endure such overwhelming grief. And with that revelation, the ghostly figure released its hold and faded into the darkness.

Relieved to be free and in control of her body once again, Mariah sat up slowly. The encounter with the "Lady in White" left her shaken. She dug for the talisman and threw it across the room. *Worthless!*

Now, after the late-night encounter with a visitor from the dark side, she was more determined than ever to solve the mystery surrounding the cowboy, the "Lady in White," and the hotel. While Kat explored the underground tunnels and Nicole shopped for souvenirs, Mariah planned to dig deeper into the history of this famous Arkansas tourist destination. Key to the 100-year-old puzzle... Eureka Springs Historical Museum.

Chapter 19
Present

Small, loose-stones littered the ground causing Kat to stumble. Pitching forward, glasses flying, she landed with a hard thud. Darkness engulfed the tunnel as the flashlight hit the dirt and rolled out of reach.

"Help!" she called out to her two accomplices. The only sounds that met her straining ears were footsteps... footsteps being quickly lost in the blackness.

Scrambling, not wanting to be left behind, Kat fumbled around on hands and knees until locating her glasses. She continued her crawl over the rocky floor, finally locating the light. She gave it a firm whack, and it flickered back to life.

She pointed the narrow beam into the darkness. A long passage stretched out ahead. She then shone the beam to the rear. The faint light of the entrance to the underground came into view, reminding her of how she had gotten into this predicament in the first place.

Kat was disappointed to find the underground excursion canceled. She followed two other disgruntled tourists to a hotel listed on the kiosk poster as a tour destination. The manager, a sympathetic listener, agreed to allow the three a quick peek at the tunnel system.

He led them to a padlocked door in the basement. Eagar to share the history of the hotel, he bragged, "This is one of the main entrances to a string of disconnected subterranean passages beneath Eureka. Our section is thought to have once connected to the Mayor's Office."

The heavy key clicked in the lock, and the door swung open. The manager pointed to a sign above the door, *Danger,*

*Do Not Enter. H*e explained the need for the strict security, "Wouldn't want some unsuspecting guest to accidentally wander in and get lost."

Before they could sneak a quick look at the famous attraction, the manager was called back to the reception desk to take a phone call. Door ajar, manager out of sight, the adventurous young man and woman didn't hesitate. They climbed into the narrow passageway and motioned for Kat to follow.

Big mistake trusting two complete strangers, Kat silently chided while picking herself up and brushing the dust from her pants. She felt the ache of bruised knees as she took a hesitant step forward. Weary of the uneven path, she reached out for the rough limestone wall. She carefully placed one foot in front of the other while following the cold stone wall with one free hand.

For several minutes, she concentrated on navigating the jagged path that lay ahead. "Where are those two idiots I followed like a lemming into this hell hole?" Kat grumbled. She pointed her light into the darkness exploring her surroundings, while her ears strained to detect any sounds of footsteps.

The musty air, heavy with the odor of decay, became more tainted the further she ventured into the underground. The foul smell made it hard to concentrate. She tried to think, but her thoughts were jumbled. She could only remember a few facts from the flyer she had picked up at the tour booth. What stood out in her mind was the system of underground passages, constructed by property owners sometime in the late 1800s, were all connected to the Basin Park Spring.

Kat continued to edge forward. In some spaces, she had to stoop to get through the passage while other sections were taller with floor beams of the buildings overhead visible twenty feet above.

She brushed aside a string of cobwebs overburdened with dust and then froze. She heard something... voices. She strained to make out the words, but there was nothing more to be heard. She called out thinking it was the missing couple, "Hey, wait for me!"

No answer.

She tried again.

Nothing.

Uneasy about continuing on her own, Kat decided to turn back. She had only taken a few steps when she was startled by a chorus of terrifying cries. She swung around, shinning her beam into the tunnel, she faced what was coming. The chaotic sounds grew louder and louder until the young man and his friend broke through the darkness.

"Run!" he urged, pushing Kat to the side.

"It's coming!" the girl yelled, close behind her friend. With her back to the stone wall, the roughness pressing into her skin, Kat shouted at the fleeing runners, "What's coming?"

Further down the tunnel came another sound. The closer it got, the more distinct the sound became... a low whispered voice. A sense of danger oozed from deep within the tunnel. It's swirled on the floor like a foggy mist ready to engulf everything in its path. Kat wrapped her arms about her chest as if to ward off an attack and clenched her quivering jaw in an effort to keep her teeth from chattering.

She swallowed hard and forced her legs to move. She shouted down the tunnel, "Is anyone there?"

Getting no answer, she tried again, "Do you need help?" The only sound that met her straining ears was the sound of her own pulse throbbing erratically.

She pushed back against the fear as she came to the unsettling realization that hidden beneath the bustling streets of Eureka Springs the underground was the perfect place for things to be done that someone might want to keep hidden. She knew it was silly, but in a town where spooky tales passed as truth, she found it easy to imagine all sorts of shadowy figures lurking in the murky depths of the darkness. So, she did the most sensible thing she could think of... she ran!

Lighting up the tunnel ahead, Kat fanatically searched for some glimpse of the couple. Finding nothing, she ran faster while struggling to keep her balance on the rugged surface.

Intense fear, so strong it prevented reason or logical thinking, seized her as the voice drew closer and closer. The whispered words now had a threatening edge to them. Above her hammering heart, she imagined she could feel each menacing footstep of the voice closing in. She could almost feel the cold, clammy grasp of wispy fingers clawing for a hold.

Really frightened now, on the verge of hysteria, she feverishly searched ahead. The yellow glow from the entrance was so faint she almost missed it. A dark figure framed in the doorway turned and yelled down the tunnel, "Hurry!" before disappearing into the light.

Reaching the entrance a few moments later, Kat didn't hesitate. She jumped.

Bent at the waist, hands-on knees, breathing hard, the couple looked up as Kat tumbled from the darkness and landed at the feet of the hotel manager.

Surprised to see the tourists in such a state, he asked, "What happened?"

"Sounds... whispered voices...," the young man said, trying to catch his breath.

Kat finished for him, "Someone... something... chased us."

"Oh, I see. The three of you went into the underground unescorted. That was foolish and dangerous. I did warn you though," he scolded, cleverly clearing the hotel of any liability.

"The tunnels are not haunted. There are no lost souls crying out for help. What spooked you was what the locals call the 'talking walls,' water from the Basin Spring. Many people claim the sound. It makes as it flows beneath the city resembles whispered voices."

Kat made eye contact with her two accomplices. They weren't buying the explanation, and neither was she. As much as she hated to admit it, there was something going on in that tunnel... something not easily explained away.

Chapter 20
Eureka Springs, Arkansas-1899

The woman rode sidesaddle into town followed by a gang of hard-looking men. She had taken one look at Tanner standing on the balcony of the Perry House and hadn't looked anywhere else. The last rays of the setting sun etched the sternly handsome face watching her watch him. He guessed it was to be expected. Once word got around about the isolated community, the chaos and disorder brought on by the boomtown's rapid growth, and most importantly, the fact the town had no jail, Ozark outlaws like her would begin to show up.

He read the message scowled across the scrap of paper again as his high heeled boots kicked up dust crossing the street, "Let's talk." He knew the writer. Known to be partial to good whiskey and gambling, he also knew where to find her.

The swinging doors brushed up against Tanner as he entered the Silver Palace already crowded with a rowdy-high spirited mix of cowboys, gamblers, thieves, and whores. Walking to the bar, he ordered a whiskey. Glass in hand, he turned and cast a wide glance around the room. Strikingly handsome, she stood out in the amber-yellow glow of the kerosene lanterns. Tight black jackets, black velvet skirts, and twin pistols, with belts of cartridges crisscrossing her hips, Belle Starr, female outlaw, waited.

Swallowing the last of the amber liquid, feeling the burn, he recalled what he had heard about this woman known to the ruthless men she traveled with as the "Bandit Queen." Her family had been sympathizers with the Southern cause during the war. Supporters of the Confederate irregulars, Belle had strapped on a six-shooter and crossed the Missouri-Kansas line disguised as a man to join Quantrill's raiders. Eventually, hooking up with Frank and Jesse James and Cole Younger, lawlessness became a way to survive.

After the War, she gained a reputation as an outlaw and a loose woman. Her ranch in Indian Territory west of Fort Smith, Arkansas, became a hideout for rustlers, horse thieves, and bank robbers. The illegal activities she organized and planned from the remote location proved profitable. When unable to buy off lawmen, she was known to seduce them into looking the other way.

Tanner had to admit the message had set him to wondering. Sliding his glass to the bartender, he made a path through the tables to where she sat. Her men, protective and loyal, tracked his every move.

Belle had seen the lone gunman walk

into the saloon. More than six feet, the width of his shoulders and the depth of his chest matched his height, around his lean waist rode a cartridge belt, from the holster protruded the butt of a pearl-handled Colt. He looked like a man who was afraid of nothing—a man who could take care of himself.

"Next to a fine horse, I admire a fine pistol," she declared in a low husky voice.

Not to be taken in by her flirty ways, Tanner questioned, "You wanted to see me?"

"I'm look'n for another rider and gun, interested?" she asked, getting down to business.

"Depends," he answered, pulling out a chair and sitting across from her.

"I plan to stop a freight train."

"Why me?" he asked. Scanning the faces of the men watching him, he said, "Looks like you have plenty of help."

"The train is carrying gold brick headed for the Denver Mint. It will be heavily guarded. Need another gun in case of trouble."

"No disrespect, Ma'am, but been on my own since I was a kid. Works best that way." he explained, turning down her offer. Pushing back his chair, tipping the black Stetson, he said, "Night Ma'am." With quick, smooth strides, Tanner left the saloon.

Early the next morning, Tanner raked back the curtain to his hotel window just in time to see Belle and her men mount up and ride out. Weeks later, he heard the Northern Pacific train was flagged down by horsemen. After the locomotive came to a halt, two masked men boarded and held guns on the engineer. The others rode up to the rail car holding the gold and ordered the guards to open up. When the men refused, the robbers simply blew the doors off with sticks of dynamite, pushed aside the dazed inhabitants, and took what they wanted.

Before riding away with the loot, the

men removed one of the iron doors from a railroad car, and using ropes dragged the door along behind them, as they made their escape on horseback.

Railroad detectives hunted for weeks, but never found the gold.

The way Tanner figured, Belle, fearing immediate pursuit from federal agents, decided to hide the gold. But the part about the door had him scratching his head. The answer came to him in a flash, *The hiding place... to conceal the hiding place.*

Riddled with caves and underground tunnels, the mountain top town of Eureka Springs was the perfect hiding place. He reasoned, *When the horsemen arrived, they entered the cave and stacked the gold against one wall. The iron door was placed over the entrance, wedged into position, and covered over with rock and brush.*

The gang attempted another train robbery a few months later, but this time things didn't go as planned. When the mail car doors rolled back, rifle fire blasted from Pinkerton Detectives hired to protect railroad interests. Bullets whistled and guns exploded as the robbers returned fire. Caught in the open, nowhere to hide, all of the gang members lay dead or dying when the smoke cleared.

Not long after, Tanner heard Starr was shot to death near Fort Smith, Arkansas, just before her 41st birthday. With her death, no one remained alive who knew the exact location of what had come to be known as the "Lost Iron Door Cache," but Tanner had a good idea where to begin the search.

Chapter 21
Present

Not sure what to expect, Nicole parted the beaded curtain. The jangle announced her arrival as she stepped into the candlelit parlor. Burning incense, pungent sweet like the scent of freshly cut flowers, wafted through the room. It floated gently on the air as if trying to calm an unseen world of restless spirits.

A middle-aged woman stood, slightly bent over a small table. With one single wave of her ringed hand, she invited her guest to sit. Nicole settled into the cushioned armchair across the table and the two exchanged formalities.

Smoothing silky waves of dark hair from her face, the gypsy woman introduced herself, "My name is Joanna. I tell fortunes, read Tarot cards, and make psychic predictions. Just as with my mother before me, I follow in the footsteps of a long line of mystics."

Impressive resume, Nicole thought, looking across the table at the woman watching her.

"What brings you here?" Joanna asked.

"Well, I'm just a curious tourist," Nicole admitted, noticing for the first time the cross on the wall and the statue of the Virgin Mary below on a metal stand. Focusing her attention back on the card reader, Nicole finished, "I've never had my fortune told; when I saw the sign in the window, I thought it was the perfect opportunity to mark it off my bucket list."

The exotic dark eyes of the card-reader missed nothing, not the tension in the young woman's face, the way she nervously chewed her lips, or the white line of a recently removed wedding ring. Guessing the visit was more than the desire to eliminate an item on a bucket list, she picked up the black star-splattered deck of cards. "Surrounded by twisted messages and lopsided facts, truth is important. Helping people discover 'truth' is something that I'm deeply passionate about."

Fascinated, Nicole watched her work the cards. The closest she had ever really come to a fortune-teller was at the county fair one year where there had been a palm-reading booth set up on the midway. She had never been tempted to visit the booth— even in fun. The supernatural was just never really her thing. She had grown up going to church, where those kinds of activities were discouraged. She had always sort of operated on the idea that it's probably better to just let destiny play itself out... until now.

"Let's begin by clearing the cards of previous energies so that nothing interferes with the clarity of your reading." Passing the cards to Nicole, the mystic instructed her to shuffle.

The deck was larger than Nicole expected; she wrapped her fingers around it, noticing the frayed gold gilt edges. *This deck has been well used,* she thought to herself. A little uneasy about what the cards might have to say about her future, she took her time. There was something soothing about the physical act of moving the cards around and to her amazement, she began to relax.

Now satisfied, she passed the deck back to Joanna. Their hands touched; their eyes met again for a few brief seconds. *Oh, my goodness! Did she just try to read my mind?* Nicole worried.

The woman, showing no emotion, placed the deck face down on the dragon-inlaid table. "Please realize, the future is not fixed. You can change things before they happen by heeding the message in the cards."

With one dramatic sweep, she spread the cards in a semicircle around the edge of the tabletop. "Draw three cards and lay

Ghosts of Perry House

them face down in a row. These cards will answer questions about your past, present, and future. As you select your card, think about a question you'd like answered."

Nicole did as instructed. She concentrated and drew three cards. Her thoughts raced, scrambling for a problem she needed help with... *death of her son... end of her marriage. No, those questions had been asked and answered months ago.*

Her thoughts turned to the late-night ghost hunt and the dark secrets surrounding the hotel. Lots of questions needing answers there, yet she hesitated. Did she really want to know, or were some things best left buried in the past? As she placed the three cards face down on the table, she tried to stop the question from forming in her mind, but it was too late. *Why does the cowboy haunt the Basin Park Hotel?*

The psychic, knowing the "question" was the hardest part for many people who sought out her guidance, patiently waited until the last card was in place, and then said, "Let's see what wisdom the cards want to share with you today."

Turning the first card, she named it, "The Five of Cups, your past." Pausing, the reader looked intently at the eighteenth-century style artwork. She tapped different parts of the picture with one long blood-red nail as she spoke, "The man looking a bit miserable represents you. He's focusing on three spilled cups at his feet oblivious to the two behind him which are still standing. He's also not seeing the bridge to his right, and the castle that lies in front of him. He's so focused on what he's lost that he doesn't see what he still has." She raised her head and looked at Nicole. "Like the man in the picture, you too have experienced great loss, immersed yourself in your sadness, and failed to see that not all was lost."

Taken by surprise, Nicole nodded her head, and answered, "Yes," but offered no details. Her struggle with death and divorce was too raw to share with a stranger.

Ghosts of Perry House

Realizing the young woman was not willing to say more, Joanna reached for the second card but did not immediately turn it over. "This card represents the present, your current problem." Her hand hovered as if detecting something untoward waiting beneath. Taking a deep breath, bracing herself, she flipped the card and whispered, "The Ten of Swords."

Nicole stared at the gruesome picture, a man lying face down with ten swords in his back. *Well,* she thought, *this sure as hell can't be a good sign.*

The mystic, visibly shaken, finally said, "A time of darkness is upon you."

"What?" Nicole demanded, eyes widening, mind on high alert.

"Something... something very, very unpleasant is coming your way."

"Whoa!" Nicole exclaimed, struggling to her feet, and backing away from the table. *This was a bad, bad idea,* she realized too late.

The fortune-teller also stood and

reached out to her client. Long fingers closed on Nicole's writs, painfully tight, restraining. Nicole had to fight the urge to pull away.

"Please, sit," the gypsy begged. "The cards are just a collection of images and have no power on their own," she tried to calm her young woman.

Nicole found no comfort in her words. Desperate to put distance between herself and the cards, she pulled free, parted the beaded curtain, and rushed to the street as if the devil himself was in pursuit.

With a deep sigh, not pleased with how the session had ended, Joanna sank back into her chair. She grasped the edge of the last card and turned it face-up on the table. "Oh, no!" she breathed in a voice, quivering with emotion as the medieval style illustration appeared; a skeleton dressed in black armor, riding a white horse... the *Death Card*.

Chapter 22
Dodge City, Kansas–1890

Tanner already had a history by the time he got to Dodge. He had nothing to live for and didn't make it a secret. There was a certain freedom; however, when you think your life is over.

The atmosphere in the Long Branch Saloon was tense with the potential for violence. All the men around the table sat stiffly, waiting for the next turn of cards and the trouble it might bring, except for Tanner. Stetson tipped back, a smile on his face; he regarded the cards in front of him: two jacks and a deuce. He picked up some bills from the pile next to him and tossed the paper into the center of the table with the rest of the pot. "I'll see that ten and raise twenty."

Most of the other players had already folded as the pot grew. The player to his left muttered, "Forget it," shoved his chair away from the table, and headed for the bar.

Tanner stared across the green felt at the young man... John Morgan's son. In his mid-twenties, dark-haired, sporting a narrow mustache, his battered hat hung behind his head from its chin strap. Tanner said, "Looks like it's down to you and me, Kid."

The kid's pile of winnings had grown considerably smaller over the course of the night. He hesitated, rubbed the deep scar that marked his cheek, then picked up some bills and tossed them into the pot. "There's your damn twenty!"

The nervous-looking dealer, swallowed, cleared his throat, and dealt a card face up to the Tanner. "That's a seven," he announced unnecessarily since everybody could see what the card was. "Still a pair of jacks showing."

Ghosts of Perry House

With expert skill, he flipped the next card in the deck to the kid. "An eight. That gives you two-pair—black Aces and black eights."

"We can all see that; damn it," the kid snapped.

Tanner let out a low whistle. "Dead Man's Hand! Aces and eights, the same five-card stud hand Hickok held when shot in the back of the head by that coward Jack McCall."

The dealer like most gamblers was superstitious, he cautioned, "Hey, Mister, speaking of the dead is bad luck!"

The kid saw through the cheap trick to rile him up and cause trouble. Too late, Lady Luck was on his side tonight. Unafraid, refusing to take the bait, he looked the cowboy in the eye. "Who the hell bids up the pot on a lousy pair of jacks? It's not good enough to beat me, and ya know it."

Tanner smiled in response. Experience had taught him that the people who have the cards are usually the ones who talk the least and the softest; those who are bluffing tend to talk loudly and give themselves away.

The young man's mouth flattened; his eyes went hard, "I know who ya are. A damn tinhorn gambler who should've been run out of town by now."

The grin on Tanner's face didn't budge, but his eyes turned hard as flint. "This game has been dealt fair and square, Son." He put his hand on the pile of bills to his left and pushed it into the middle of the table. "And I reckon I'm all in." Tanner settled back into his seat.

"I'm not goin' to let ya bluff me!" The kid pushed his remaining money into the pile at the center of the table. "I'm goin' to call, ya." He turned over his hole card, which was a seven. "My aces and eights beat your two jacks," he announced reaching for the pot.

"Hold on," Tanner demanded as he flipped over his hole card, a jack. "Three of a kind always beats two-pair."

Ghosts of Perry House

The kid's face grew dark with anger as he stared at the cards. His breath hissed between clenched teeth. He angrily shoved his chair back and stood.

Tanner's right hand moved closer to the gun at his hip. Everybody in the saloon had started edging away. The lace and fringed serving girls ducked behind cover. In a matter of moments, nobody was anywhere near the two players.

The kid uttered a curse and clawed the six-shooter at his hip. He started to lift the gun-only to stop short as he found himself staring down the barrel of Tanner's Colt.

Tanner advised, "Saddle your horse and ride on out. Hanging around here is going to get you killed!"

Slowly replacing his gun, hands held to his sides, the kid backed from the saloon.

Tanner slugged back his drink while scooping the bills from the table. Scrapping the chair back, he stood and stuffed the winnings in one of his pants pockets. He walked out into the night, leaving the batwing doors swinging.

Across the street, three men watched. And, when he started down the street, they walked along keeping pace with him from the other side. One was the kid. Tanner paid them no mind as he kept walking. At the end of the street was the livery and across was the dry goods store and beyond nothing else. It was obvious where he was headed.

At the end of the street, he stopped. The three men stopped. Tanner stepped off the boardwalk and onto the dirt street. He walked straight across toward the three men.

"I want my money!" the kid shouted.

Tanner kept walking. The kid hadn't expected it. He wasn't sure what he should do.

"Hey, Mister, what the hell ya doin'?" he asked.

"I'm going to kill you," Tanner said. He

Ghosts of Perry House

didn't speak very loudly, but the three heard, and his steady voice made them flinch back a half step.

Tanner could feel the steady rhythm of his heart. He felt the weight of the Colt in his belt. He opened his hands wide and let them relax at his sides. He was close now. If the kid was going to make his move, he'd need to do it soon, before Tanner was on top of him. The kid knew it and went for his gun. With one fluid motion, Tanner drew and fired, the Colt bucking slightly as the hammer fell. The shot hit the kid before his hand reached the butt of the six-shooter.

One of the kid's friends managed to get a shot off hitting Tanner in the right arm. Without any pause, Tanner shot the two men. Then there was silence. In the utter stillness, the smell of gun powdered was thick. Tanner reloaded, walked to each man to make sure they were dead. Holstering the Colt, he walked on to the livery.

Chapter 23
Present

Answers... Mariah needed answers, and the Eureka Springs Historical Museum, nestled in the heart of the downtown district, was a good place to start. Hating long lines, she had arrived mid-morning when most sightseers were still eating breakfast and planning their day. She eagerly pushed open the door and stepped into the newly restored 100-year-old structure known as the Calif House.

The cashier, a friendly woman in her mid-fifties took the five-dollar donation and passed Mariah a map in exchange. She politely invited Mariah to take the self-guided tour of official documents, unique artifacts,

Ghosts of Perry House

and turn-of-the-century photographs housed in the building.

"Our recently renovated main floor includes temporary and permanent displays. Second floor, gallery featuring local artists," she explained, pointing to the wooden staircase.

"Thank you," Mariah said, sidestepping a couple admiring jewelry by local artists at the souvenir counter.

She unfolded the map and briefly scanned a color-coded diagram. From the drawing, Mariah came to the conclusion that this wasn't going to be a quick in-and-out investigation but would involve several hours of digging through layers of history to uncover the truth.

Refolding the map, she tucked it into a back pocket. She entered the exhibit hall not knowing what she was looking for but hoping to find something... anything that would shed light on the mysterious happenings at 12 Spring Street. A few feet within the entrance, something unexpected happened. A sudden cold shiver shot up her spine, and her chest tightened, leaving Mariah breathless. She stopped. Physical senses heightened, she cleared her mind and patiently waited to see what came to her. And then, oh-so-gently, the air stirred. An intuitive tug almost like having a magnet in her gut pulled Mariah forward.

She put logic aside and went with her intuition, an internal compass she had learned to trust. The built-in GPS directed her to a line of bright yellow arrows painted on the wooden floor.

Following the markings to the first presentation of artifacts, a floor-to-ceiling glass case, she stood for a moment. Her gaze swept the well-arranged assortment of buckskin clothing, woven baskets, clay fashioned pottery, and handcrafted weapons. Her attention was quickly captured by two colorful oil paintings. The first, a tribal chieftain, pipe in one hand, tomahawk in the other; his body wrapped in a huge Mackinaw blanket stood tall and proud.

Beneath the picture, a plaque read: "The Osage tribe, fierce protectors of their land, claimed the vast Ozark Region." The other painting, titled *Scared Ground,* depicted several different tribes peacefully camped along the banks of a big spring.

Her mind scrambled, connecting what she had learned to what she knew. She came to a startling conclusion; the unusual events taking place at the park and the hotel were not related. The shadowy beings, darting around the Basin Spring Park, were linked to the Osage Tribe. She believed it was possible, in death as in life, they guarded the healing waters.

The supernatural activity inside the hotel was a different matter altogether. She was certain the apparitions she had seen at the hotel window were not linked to the park. But, instead, the three spirits were trapped inside the property; bound to the location by some violent or tragic event in the building's past.

The nagging psychic tug urged her to

move on to a full-size diorama, a hand-painted mountainous scene with clouds floating above. At the center of the three-dimensional display stood a life-like replica of a man: white-headed, dressed in a rumpled black suit, dipping a cup into a large pool of water at the edge of a forest. Stacked at his feet were several glass bottles labeled *Jackson's Eye Water.*

Sound effects, gentle rustling of tree leaves and soft chirruping of birds, made the nature scene astonishingly realistic. Mariah folded her arms, shook her head. *Just amazing. I can almost feel the breeze.*

Curious, she pushed a red button at the listening station to activate the audio portion of the exhibit. "In 1854, Dr. Alvah Jackson stumbled upon the great spring. He bottled the water and began selling it as a cure for eye ailments," the recorded voice announced.

At the end of the recording, she assessed the scene one last time: the

Ghosts of Perry House

man, the spring, the bottles. *Did I miss anything?* she wondered.

Finding nothing, she allowed the arrows to guide her to an area of the museum devoted to the Civil War. Two full-bodied male mannequins, dressed in worn and tattered uniforms, one Union and the other Confederate, were positioned in front of a triple-panel divider. Studying the information, Mariah gathered the town's reputation as a health resort had its origins in the war. Images on each panel detailed the treatment of the sick and wounded from both sides. Hundreds of men, many just skin and bones, bathed in and drank from the healing spring. A sampling of jugs, tin cups, and ladles used to take the "liquid cure" hung from pegs attached to the wooden frame of the divider.

Mariah mulled over what she had learned so far, searching for a thread of information that would connect the ghosts of the Basin Park Hotel with the dreadful conflict. Giving up, she walked on, joining a small crowd at a glass wall case. Inside, wanted posters, yellowed with age, immortalized some of the most notorious outlaw-heroes, bushwhackers, and vigilantly groups of the Ozarks. She was familiar with several of the names: Jesse and Frank James, Cole and Bob Younger, and Belle Starr. She had spent many weekends with her grandpa binge-watching old westerns on what he liked to call "Saddle up Saturday." But the last poster in the line-up, a drawing of several men wearing bizarre horned masks, was new to her.

"Hum,... Bald Knobbers," the man next to her recited the name from the poster.

The curator, who had organized the new collection, left her desk and approached the group. "Faces like devils," she said, pointing to the masked men.

"What?" Mariah asked.

"Bald Knobbers!" she responded, emphasizing the odd-sounding name. "Self-appointed citizens who decided to take the law into their own hands. The group got its

Ghosts of Perry House

name from the grassy summits of the nearby mountains where they were known to hold secret meetings."

"You see," she continued, "the Ozarks has a peculiar history. After the Civil War, it was a lawless wasteland, ne'er do wells like Jessie and Frank James and vigilante groups like the Bald Knobbers emerged to fill the void of authority. Some mountain people saw them as righteous folk heroes; others regarded them as murderous thugs."

The curator had spent many late nights researching, developing, and organizing the new collection, and was more than happy to take the time to share her considerable knowledge. She pointed to a poster advertising a $5,000-per-man-bounty for the James gang and explained, "In a time when mass media didn't exist, this was the best bet for law enforcement in getting the public's attention."

The members of the small group patiently listened before wandering off to explore what remained of the main floor exhibits. Mariah stayed. She directed her gaze back to the line of wanted posters. Disappointed, the one face she hoped to find was missing.

Well, doesn't mean he wasn't an outlaw, she reasoned.

Ready to continue her search, she looked around for the next stop on the history tour. She was surprised to find the room, oddly silent, and nearly deserted. Lost in the past, she had stayed at the museum longer than intended. Rummaging in her purse, nervous fingers finally snagged the phone. She checked the time.

The curator noticed and cautioned, "Oh, you don't want to leave before seeing the last exhibit, *Fires-The Big Ones!*"

Fires! Mariah's head jerked up. That one word left her feeling dizzy and lightheaded. The air began to vibrate with invisible energy, tickling the hairs on both arms. She guessed whatever she was

Ghosts of Perry House

supposed to discover was near, and it wanted to be found.

She slow-walked past several leather fire buckets piled around a red and gold horse-drawn fire engine. She spotted a timeline of the 1800s painted on the wall of the exhibit. She inched forward to get a better look. Each branch of the graph was dedicated to one of the four great fires credited with scorching the mountainsides and destroying most of the wooden framed structures of the town. With one slender finger, she traced the dark line to each date, stopping at 1890. She skimmed the information beneath the date. "Forty-five homes and many businesses along Spring Street were consumed in the fire which originated at the Perry House Hotel."

Her finger guided, by an unseen force, glided effortlessly along the line to a striking black and white photography labeled, *Perry House*. The image quivered with dark energy.

"This is it," Mariah whispered under her breath.

She studied the Victorian citizens decked in their finery lounging on the third-floor balcony and came face to face with the man she was seeking. Hat in hand, six-shooter strapped to his waist stood the cowboy. Next to him, a woman held the hand of a child. Solemn, unsmiling, the three stared out onto the street.

Chapter 24
Eureka Springs, Arkansas-1890

He was sitting in the hotel lobby the first time he saw her. Hearing the hoofbeats and the rattle of stagecoach wheels approaching, he looked up from his newspaper and out the window. The coach swayed and bounced up-and-down along the bumpy dirt street.

"Whoa!" cried the driver. The coach slowed and then stopped in front of the sixty-room Perry House, the most up-to-date and fashionable hostelry in Eureka Springs. "Easy now," he cautioned the six quivering and snorting horses.

Setting the brake, he looped the reins around the handle and then climbed down to the street some seven feet below. He opened the coach door and offered a helping hand to one of two passengers. A gloved hand accepted his offer. Gathering her skirt with the other, the young woman carefully stepped down to the street revealing a slim ankle. She pushed back a strand of honey-blonde hair and then straightened her hat. While brushing the dust from her skirt, the driver swung a small girl dressed in yellow from the coach, setting her long, cornsilk-colored braids swing.

The man riding shotgun, tossed the woman's trunk to the hotel porter as the driver climbed back to his seat. He snapped the reins over the backs of the horses. Then yelled, "Yee-ah!" The stagecoach lurched and rolled on.

Tanner watched the woman smile down at the child and gently take the small hand in hers. The two entered the hotel and walked to the registration desk.

A damn good-looking woman, Tanner thought. *Fair skin, slender waist, and nicely rounded breasts.* Tanner was quick to note, he wasn't the only male following the sway of the woman's hips in the full skirt as she swept through the lobby and up the stairs with the child.

Tanner stood, stretched, and then making up his mind, he headed for the stairs. Keeping his distance, not wanting to cause alarm, he followed. Rounding the corner of the third floor, he almost collided with the young girl. The mother, struggling with the gold room key, looked up.

The kid's gaze fastened on Tanner's gun. "Are you an outlaw?" she inquired bluntly.

"I used to be," he answered, surprising her.

"My goodness," the woman remarked, pulling her daughter close. In the glow of the gaslights, gun riding low on his right hip, gunslinger fashion, he looked dangerous.

"You're safe with me Ma'am," he assured her. "Let me help you with the door," he suggested.

She hesitated and then handed over the key. Tanner stepped close leaving little space between them. He caught the scent of her... fresh and womanly as he accepted the key.

She blushed. For a moment, she thought he was going to kiss her, his face was so very close to hers... but he didn't.

Steel-gray eyes glinted with mischief as the lock clicked, and he pushed the door open. He stood back politely allowing the woman to guide the young girl into the room. He wanted to reach out and touch the smooth skin of her cheek with the back of his fingers; he held back not wanting to frighten her with the bold move.

Turning to face him, she simply said, "Thank you."

"Goodnight, Ma'am," Tanner said, tipping his hat and flashing a grin.

She blushed again, oddly flustered.

As Tanner walked further down the hall to room 310, he considered the fire he glimpsed in the woman's eyes before she closed and locked the door. He wondered, *What kind of man would let a woman like that wander so far from home?*

Tanner took it slow and easy over the next few weeks. First, he found out from the desk clerk, Mrs. Elisabeth Warren and her daughter, Sarah, were from back East. Next, he made a point of being around when the two ventured from their room. Meeting in the hallway or in passing on the stairs, Tanner would tip his hat with a smile that never failed to bring a hint of pink to pale cheeks.

Today, finding Elisabeth, he didn't think of her as Mrs. Warren, sitting in the lobby with Sarah at her side, he decides to make his move. He confidently strolled to the settee across from the easy chair where she sat.

"Good morning, Ma'am," he said. Tanner casually picked up and opened the discarded newspaper before sitting. Scanning the page, he pretended interest in what he found there.

"Good morning," she answered, taking a sip from the china cup.

"We're going to the bathhouse at 10 o'clock," Sarah announced, leaving her mother's side to sit on the red velvet cushion next to him. Young and innocent, she had come to trust the friendly man with the gun. "I was sick all winter, and Dr. Goodman says the water will help me get my strength back."

Tanner put his paper to the side. His fingers fished around and finally pulled the silver timepiece from his vest pocket. Curious, Sarah leaned close to get a better look. Tanner smiled, snapping the lid, and replacing the timepiece, he said, "It's almost time for your bath, little one."

"There are some pretty rowdy strangers in town right now," he said, turning his gaze on Elizabeth. "May I escort you and Sarah?"

Taken by surprise, the woman hesitated before answering. "How do you know my name, Mister…?" then paused.

"Tanner... just Tanner, Ma'am." He introduced himself with a tip of his Stetson, and then explained how he discovered her name. "Desk clerk; he's a real obliging feller for the right price," he said, standing and putting out his hand.

Elisabeth considered the offer. She felt safe with this man; even though she knew from the gun on his hip and his direct manner, he was very dangerous. It might not be a bad thing to have him at her side if there was trouble.

"Very, well,... Tanner," she agreed, taking his outstretched hand and rising from the chair. Conscious of the warm sensation of her hand in his strong calloused one, she shyly tugged free.

Elizabeth briefly looked down on her daughter still seated, then turned her clear blue eyes on him. "Sarah and I would very much like for you to accompany us this morning," she said, tenderly replacing his hand with that of her daughter's smaller one.

In that moment something inside Tanner changed. The numbness he felt gave way to yearning... a longing for this woman and for a different kind of life.

Chapter 25
Basin Park, Eureka Springs-1890

Tanner paused at the Basin Spring Park arched gateway. His patience had finally paid off. His reward, her trust. A smile curved his lips as he tucked her arm around his. They began their nightly evening stroll in silence. The cobblestones wove a path through lush greenery. The summer breeze died, leaves creased to rustle, even the rumble of wagon wheels and the beat of horse hooves was absent. For the next few moments, the focus of his attention was the crunch of dried twigs beneath his boot heels.

His feelings for her had caused him to ponder his life. *Who am I? What have I become: outlaw,... gunfighter,... cold-blooded killer?* Although he was unsure of the answers, he was sure of one thing; the innocent boy of his childhood had been slain by ruthless marauders and left to rot on the Kansas prairie. The wound went deep. In the depths of horror and despair, the darkened path was the one he chose. Over time, the ache of loss and loneness became part of him, and no amount of hate or revenge was able to drive out the darkness.

Then she had come into his life. She brought light to the darkness that welled up within him. She filled up the profound emptiness of his life. If he could stop life for a while, he would stop here; he found quite to his surprise, that he was happy. He smiled, transforming the harsh plains of his face. In that moment, Tanner realized the greatest thing in life was to love and—to be loved in return.

Tanner had his mindset on her, but it would take money. He was more determined than ever to find the Banded

Queen's stash of gold; he just needed a little more time.

He paused under the low hanging branches of an oak tree and turned to her. She stared up at him, caught by the color of his eyes, steel-gray, startling against the sunbaked face. Crisp blond hair curled out from beneath the rim of his dark Stetson. The white linen shirt tucked into denim pants did little to conceal the male strength of his body. From his waist hung a gun belt with a pearl handle Colt strapped to his leg.

Tanner measured her for an unsmiling moment, then nodded abruptly. "Still want to come with me?"

"Yes," she answered quickly.

His long finger tilted her chin up.

She met his eyes without blinking.

Slowly he bent to take her lips. Gentilly, he moved over her mouth. His arms closed around her slender waist while he kissed her with hunger as deep as the spring that ran beneath the park. When he finally lifted his mouth, he searched her face, breathing deep.

At last, voice husky, almost hard, he said, "Alright."

Chapter 26
Present

The Lucky 7 Bar was packed. Laugher from within could be felt outside where Nicole and Mariah stood. The tinkle on tinkle of glass, the cool clink of ice, and the fizz of soda greeted them at the entrance. The bartender was busy but managed a quick welcoming wink.

Tourists seemed to be the primary patrons, which meant great company and conversation. Three billiard tables took up the right-hand side of the room. Several long tables on the other side were occupied by a wedding party. Smaller black tables were filled by people in party mode, having a good time.

At one, littered with mangled lime

wedges, salt crystals, and empty glasses sat Kat downing her third tequila shot. Nicole and Mariah joined her, signaling the bartender for another round. When the drinks arrived, Mariah finished hers, licked the salt from her fist, and bit into the lime. "How was underground Eureka?"

Nicole noticed the white tape holding Kat's glasses, "Who'd you piss off on the tunnel tour?"

Seconds ticked by. *Is omitting the truth the same as lying*, Kat wondered. Avoiding eye contact, deciding to take the narrow road between truth and deception, she admitted, "Not what I expected."

Mariah frowned and challenged Kat, "So-o-o?"

"Okay... Okay. I kind of took a self-guided tour with two other tourists, a young couple."

"And...," Nicole prompted, pointing to the scratched lenses and tapped earpiece.

Outnumbered, in damage control mode, Kat searched for the right words before confessing. "The tunnel was dark, rocky, and... well, I tripped, hence the amateur repair job. I hate to admit it, but I could've used a good dousing of that calming lavender water you've been slathering all over your body when you think no one is watching."

The corners of Nicole's mouth turned up and her eyes sparkled. "Which I interpret as, it was really freaky, and you were scared as hell!" Both Nicole and Mariah laughed out loud at the look on Kat's face.

"For a nonbeliever, it appears our ghost denier got a healthy dose of fear on her self-guided tour."

Eager to direct the inquisition away from underground Eureka, Kat turned to her sister. "Your turn."

Nicole cringed as Mariah and Kat trained their eyes on her. Silence stretched as seconds ticked by. Should she reveal her experience with the card reader? Kat wouldn't approve, which would lead to an argument and hurt feelings. Growing up it was made very plain to the two sisters that psychics were evil and horoscopes, tarot cards, and palm readings were taboo. Finally, she opted for safe, a half-truth. "Wandered around the shops, ate lunch, and sat in the park where tourists had gathered to listen to street musicians. They are quite good. Really."

"Un-huh," Kat leaned back in her chair and regarded her sister. She sensed there was more to tell but didn't push. Nicole was stubborn and pushing wouldn't get answers.

Not waiting to be asked, impatient to share her discovery, Mariah blurted out, "I think I found a photograph of the cowboy."

"What?" Nicole asked, doing a double take of her friend.

"Impossible, we don't even know his name," Kat insisted.

"No, I'm serious. I spent most of the day checking out the different displays. They have everything about the history of the town—documents, artifacts, and old photographs. I was ready to give up and leave when the museum curator steered me to the last exhibit. Get this... it was an illustrated timeline of the four fires that swept through Eureka Springs during the late 1800s. The 1890 date displayed a picture of the Perry House Hotel before it burned. On the third-floor balcony, a cowboy in a white canvas duster stood by a woman and little girl."

"And...?" Mariah stretched out the word to make a point.

"Don't you see? This proves the cowboy stayed at the hotel during the time of the last fire. He is standing on the third-floor balcony. The very floor where all the guests perished in the fire. The woman in white and the little girl that haunt the third floor are standing beside him."

"At best, circumstantial evidence. No names. No date. That could be a photograph of anyone. Don't think it would hold up in a court of law," Kat pointed out.

"We'll never be able to prove 100% that this is a picture of the ghosts that haunt the Basin Park Hotel. All records were destroyed in the fire along with the building and most of the town. But the photograph confirms it for me. Mystery solved; case closed."

Standing she said, "Now let's get moving. I have reservations for three at the Intrigue Theater."

Chapter 27
Present

The three women sat side-by-side in the small, intimate theater which had been cleverly converted from a century-old church. The high ceilings of the Intrigue Theater supported brilliant crystal chandeliers and the seating was surrounded by the original stained-glass windows. The venue exuded an aura of mystery.

"I saw these guys compete on some T.V. show with a mind-reading monkey. They had to pull off their trick in front of professional magicians, who were the judges," Mariah shared.

"Did they fool the judges?" Nicole asked.

"No, but the whole act was hilarious!"

"This should be a great show then. You have to be damn good just to get an appearance on national T.V," Kat pointed out.

As the lights dimmed, the audience fell silent. A young man parted the red velvet curtain and stepped forward. "Welcome to an evening of mystery and intrigue with Sean-Paul the Illusionist and Juliana Fay the Ghost Talker—featuring special guests from the other side. Their performance will challenge your reality, engage your senses, and baffle even the most skeptical minds! Communicating with ghosts, casting voodoo spells, and magic that defies gravity are just a few of the mysteries that will be explored and demonstrated by the husband-wife duo. So, sit back and enjoy the show." The announcer disappeared; the opening curtains revealed the performers.

The entertainers were decked out in lavish costumes. Sean-Paul was obviously inspired by the Golden Age of Magic where magicians had amazed their Victorian spectators. He wore a gold single-breasted vest that flashed beneath a knee-length black form-fitting jacket. His wife, Juliana, dressed in more revealing attire, one that enhanced her striking figure and fair complexion. It could be described as Vegas showgirl style, but it paired nicely with her partner's.

The duo took the up-close personal approach and left the stage to interact with the audience. Handsome, blue-eyed Sean-Paul started with the silver spoon trick. A row of witnesses confirmed that it was indeed a solid spoon. He then rested the spoon between two fingers, concentrated, and slowly rubbed his fingers up and down the handle. It began to bend before their eyes. The crowd was awed and applauded as he moved on to his next sleight of hand.

"How'd he do that?" Nicole asked, eyes bright, cheeks flushed.

After untangling three, large-intertwined rings, pulling a few card tricks, and making objects disappear and reappear, the performance moved back to center stage for parlor magic. Four volunteers were invited to form a circle and place both hands on a round, wooden table. They were directed to focus all thoughts on their hands. Within seconds, the table shook slightly as if in protest. The participants were encouraged to keep their thoughts centered.

Like a wild bronco trying to throw its rider, the table bucked, kicked, and tested its restraints. The volunteers struggled but to no avail for the table rose and now hung a couple of feet in the air. Two of the helpers, visibly shaken, jerked back nervously. At this point, Sean-Paul assisted the group by dramatically placing both hands on the tabletop. Wrestling for control, he finally brought the rebellious piece of furniture back to the stage. Spontaneous approval erupted and echoed throughout and then softly died away.

The show continued with another aide; a man from the first row was called on stage and blindfolded. The illusionist cut a few strands of hair from the unsuspecting man's head and wrapped them around the head of a small cloth figure suspiciously resembling a voodoo doll.

Using a gold-handled cane, he explained, "I will touch you with my cane. I want you to point to the place where you feel the nudge." Sean-Paul proceeded to gently tap the man several times about his upper body. Each time, the man correctly pointed to where he had been touched. Next, he put down his cane and picked up the burlap doll. One after another, he stuck long straight pins in the doll until it looked like a seamstress's pincushion. To the astonishment of the viewers, the part of the body the man identified as feeling the poke perfectly matched each pin stick of the doll.

Mariah exchanged looks with the two sisters. "Now that was bizarre!"

"Magic defies logic," Nicole said.

Kat dismissed Nicole's explanation.

"That wasn't magic. That was a well-executed illusion. But how in the hell did he pull it off?"

Amid boisterous applause, the blindfold was removed, and the baffled man returned to his seat. The lights went up, signaling the end of the first half of the show; while the man's wife and children explained what had happened on stage. "For real, Dad, he controlled you with a voodoo doll and stick pins!"

"I'm going to do a bathroom trick, if you two want to join me," Kat declared.

Nicole chimed in, "If it involves disappearing water, I can do the same trick. Let's go!"

Mariah looked over at her companions. "I need to stretch my legs; I'm going to check out the souvenirs while you two work your special brand of magic."

Guests stood in line to pay for their merchandise. Autographed photos of Sean-Paul and Juliana Fay seemed to be the hot item, but several held crystal pendants. A box of magic coin and card tricks became Mariah's new twenty-dollar prize.

She met up with her friends as they exited the little girl's room. "Look what I got." She thrust the kit in front of them and disclosed, "This reminds me of when I was a kid. Grandpa used to make a coin appear behind my ear. You never know, I might just be a magician myself before the night's over!"

"Magic makes me feel good, I can leave the world of reality and for a while, live in the pretend one," Nicole confessed. Finding it hard to hold the unblinking stare of her sister, she quickly exclaimed, "Hey, the lights are dimming. Come on; I hope we didn't lose our seats!"

Kat gave Mariah a concerned glance, at Nicole's comment. She whispered, "I'm worried about her." Mariah nodded, and the pair settled into their original third-row seats.

Ghost Talker, Juliana Fay, was now

center stage with her husband, who was making a big show of placing a blindfolding over her eyes. She enlightened the spectators, "I hear the voices of the dead; people like me are sensitive to the vibrations of the spirit world. I think of it like an old radio where the listener is attempting to tune into the station they want to hear."

As a man from the audience checked the blindfold's security and then returned to his seat, Sean-Paul used his handheld microphone to instruct theater guests. "Take out an item from your purse or wallet. With the help of the spirits, Juliana will identify and give details about what you have selected."

Skeptics rummaged through their belongings for items that would challenge her ability. Mariah rubbed the buckeye, but let it remain hidden in her pocket. Juliana stood like a member of the Royal Guard seemingly opening her mind to make a connection with the spirit realm. Sean-

Paul randomly selected individuals. One-by-one, she described the items including the number of people in a family photograph and a smoker's brand of cigarettes.

Puzzled, Kat turned to her sister, "How is she doing this?"

Nicole shook her head, "No idea! I only know, blindfolded, she got 100% of the items correct."

A woman behind Kat loudly proclaimed, "Now I know you're authentic because there's no way you could've known that!" after Juliana Fay correctly identified the last four digits of her credit card.

Nicole gasped, "She has to be getting messages from the spirit world. It has to be some sort of supernatural magic power because she is revealing things about the audience that she has no earthly way of knowing."

With a healthy dose of respect, mixed with a little bit of fear, Kat wondered, *How can she possibly know these things?*

From the aisle, Sean-Paul motioned Mariah to stand. Turning to his wife on stage he asked, "What's she holding?"

"A talisman, it's in her pocket."

"What is the talisman?" Mariah asked convinced that there was no way anyone could know.

Without hesitation, Juliana clarified, "I believe it's a large round seed of some sort,... dark brown in color. Some people carry them for good luck."

Mariah's jaw dropped as she produced and revealed the buckeye. Before anyone could react to the revelation, Juliana said, "I'm getting a message." Hand to her ear signaled she was listening to a voice that only she could hear. "It's for someone sitting near the one holding the buckeye. Nikki... maybe."

"Nicole!" shouted Kat and Mariah in unison.

Undisturbed by the outburst, the Ghost Talker continued her silent conversation with the visiting spirit. Finally, she spoke.

"Yes, the name is Nicole. The message is from Zack."

Visibly shaken, Nicole listened intently, hoping for words of comfort from the other side.

Voice soft, filled with compassion, the message from the other side continued, "He wants Mamma to know he isn't sick anymore, and he's happy."

The performance had taken on a serious tone. There was no denying that Juliana had clairaudient powers. Nicole smiled through her tears. Kat hugged her close as Mariah patted her hand. A sympathizing audience member came over to console, offering a handful of tissues.

Eyes were back on the Juliana Fay as she raised her hand and tilted her head in an effort to hear more. "Someone in the third row is holding a key... a gold key."

Kat didn't answer; she squirmed a bit and hoped the message wasn't for her.

The ghost channeler was now

involved in a whispered back and forth conversation with the spirit world. At last, she nodded and spoke directly to the spirits. "Yes," she answered confirming she understood the silent query.

Anticipation held the crowd spellbound. Then the spirits spoke through the Ghost Talker, "Life and death are one thread, the same line viewed from different sides."

She stopped, removed her blindfold, and sought out the guardian of the key. Making eye contact with Kat, Juliana Fay warned, "Room 310... the line between the living and the dead... is forever blurred."

Chapter 28
Present

Kat and Mariah stepped into the hallway, shutting the door to room 310. In front, the hall ran draped in shadows. At their backs, the moonlight came in through the window of the emergency exit door and fell in bright patches on the carpet.

Feeling daring and hoping to discover more about who or what resided in the haunted hotel, Mariah shot over her shoulder, "Come on!"

"I'm right behind you," Kat said, eager to get started.

Kat felt overcome with curiosity. Skeptical, maybe even cynical, before this trip, she would've said she didn't believe in the paranormal. Now, she wasn't so sure.

"Follow the science" had always been her thinking about the supernatural. But there was no settle science when it came to the paranormal, and there just wasn't a logical explanation for what she had encountered in the spooky underground tunnels of the town. Frustrated, she gave herself a good mental shake. *Maybe some places held on to good or bad energies, and maybe that was what a person felt in a place like the Basin Park Hotel.*

Staying on the third floor, reportedly the center of the hotel's paranormal phenomena, provided her the perfect opportunity to learn more. So, when Nicole declined the offer, Kat had agreed to accompany Mariah on her late-night "tour of discovery." She hoped something would happen, something she could be sure was more than just a creepy feeling.

Kat caught up with Mariah as she rounded the corner. Shadows flitted noiselessly right and left as the two began walking forward, close, arms by their

Ghosts of Perry House

sides. The empty hall was straight and windowless with rooms on each side. Behind the doors, in darkened rooms, guests slept unaware and unconcerned.

Kat glanced side-to-side thinking that perhaps they would get lucky and see or hear something unusual. They didn't have to wait long.

"Hey, check this out," she said shoving her phone in Mariah's face. I downloaded the ghost hunting app recommended by Stemmons last night.

Interested, Mariah took a closer look at the phone screen. "What does it do?"

"It's an EVP detector, or for us amateur ghost hunters, Electronic Voice Phenomena detector. The app records grunts, words, or even simple sentences that cannot be detected by the human ear and then displays them on the phone screen. When the bars on the graph are green and moving up and down the app is recording."

"Please, tell me you didn't pay for that download," Mariah begged. "It's probably just a word generator! It spits out random words and names that make no sense. It's just a waste of time!"

"Well, let's just see about that." Kat swiped the screen with one finger activating the app. The bars on the voice graph flashed green and started moving up and down in no particular order. The two waited in silence for the spirits to come through; eyes following the movement of the graph bars. Nothing.

Discouraged, Kat opened her mouth ready to admit the app was a mistake when the phone began to vibrate in her hand. The bars on the graph lit up, moving faster and faster. Letters as if typed by invisible fingers appeared one at a time at the bottom of the screen, forming words. "Leave Now. Bad Man."

Eyes wide, Kat and Mariah studied the screen then each other.

Mariah stiffened at the message and demanded, "Turn that thing off!"

As Kat punched the off button on the

Ghosts of Perry House

side of her phone a sudden cold blast of air rushed through the hall. She shivered from the chill. She could see Mariah's breath, each exhale sent forth a small white cloud.

At the same time, Mariah's phone alarm beeped. "It's beginning," she whispered, pulling the cell from her back pocket. She noted the time. "Midnight, the Witching Hour." Slipping the phone back in place, she continued, "Whatever boundaries separate the world of the living form the world of the dead are now at their weakest. If anything is going to happen tonight, it will happen soon."

At that moment, Kat was not watching or listening to Mariah but had turned her head toward the darkened hallway at their backs. She thought she had heard something. The sound of rushing feet, heavy, and very swift.

"Shhhh," Kat demanded, putting a finger to her lips.

Silence hung on the air, eerily unnatural. It lingered, thick and heavy, like a woolen blanket. Nicole strained to hear whatever Kat had heard. Searching the shadows, detecting nothing, she turned to find Kat ashen-pale and shaking. Reaching for Kat's arm, she gave it a squeeze. "Well, whatever it was, it's gone now, so let's keep going."

"It still feels like something is at our backs watching, waiting for an opportunity," Kate explained as both turned to continue their investigation.

On high alert now, anticipating the unexpected, they slow-walked the next half a dozen steps with care. Nearing the end of the hallway, the furthest door from them crept open, allowing an amber glow to fall like a narrow stream across the carpet to the opposite wall. Their minds told them not to move, but their bodies refused to obey. Irresistible and dangerous, they were drawn closer and closer to the light like moths to a flame.

The two hesitated at the room entrance. Then stepping closer, they

Ghosts of Perry House

dared to look inside. For a second, Kat and Mariah remained stock still. Facing them, stood the figure of a woman, at her side, a young girl. Woman and child remained motionless for the space of a single second. Then the light flickered off, and they were gone.

"Guests... or ghosts?" Kat asked her friend, struggling to get the words out, eyes glued to the empty darkness framed in the doorway.

Before Mariah could answer, the door slammed shut with a dull thud causing the ghost hunters to jump back. Propped up by the wall, the two stood frozen in time. The seconds ticked by.

Hand to mouth, Kat stifled the scream threatening to escape.

All pretense of bravery lost, Mariah grabbed Kat's hand and bolted for the way they came.

"Let's get the hell out of here!" commanded the voice at Kat's elbow which she hardly recognized as Mariah's.

Chapter 29
Eureka Springs–1890

"**Fire!** Fire!" the alarm sounded up and down the hall.

Tanner awoke disoriented, not understanding. He barely remembered falling asleep. After an afternoon of searching the tunnels and a night of drinking and gambling, he had stumbled to bed not even removing his boots.

The first thing he noticed was the yellow-orange glow coming from the window. Jumping up, he checked his timepiece, the hands pointed straight up. Midnight, he noted, yanking back the curtain. "What the hell?"

Fire was everywhere; it was devouring everything in its path. In hopes of saving the screaming horses trapped in the stable, someone had opened the doors and drove them into the street. Tanner was relieved that his gelding was one of the animals he saw racing for safety.

"Oh, God—no!" he begged in desperation as he watched the destruction of the town. The tightly packed wooden structures could not withstand the red and yellow fury as it swept through the streets. Quicker and quicker the infernos advanced, gaining strength. As Tanner turned from the horrific scene, the Perry House was engulfed in a blazing inferno. "Elizabeth... Sarah!" he whispered with a gut-wrenching groan.

His body exploded into action. He strapped on the Colt and struggled into the white canvas duster. He would need the extra protection against what awaited him in the hall.

Grabbing the Stetson from the bed, he opened the door to chaos. The screams and cries of the women mingled, with the wailing of children, and the shouts of men. Black smoke billowed into the heated air, so thick that it was difficult to breathe. Flames leaped and danced, terrorizing half-dressed guests fleeing their rooms while orange blazes blew out windows and sent red horizontal jets out into the night.

The burn is too quick and too ferocious for the firefighters to get here in time. Nobody will likely survive, he thought. Tanner knew If he didn't want to be trapped in this burning hellhole, he would have to fight his way through the smoky firestorm.

Girm-faced, he tugged the bandanna from his neck up, covering mouth and nose. He groped his way through the fog of smoke for what seemed like an eternity finally reaching Elizabeth's room.

She answered his pounding, in a white dressing gown with Sarah at her side. Hair loose about her shoulders and panic in her eyes, she went willingly into his arms. He briefly brushed his lips across her temple and then bent and scooped up Sarah. Her arms wrapped tightly around his neck as she buried her small, frightened face in his shoulder. Grabbing Elizabeth tight around the waist, he headed for the stairs.

Please, this can't be the end not when I've just found something worth living for, he prayed as smoke and ash rained down into their hair and eyes. But it was too late; flames were already greedily licking at the walls and blocking any chance of escape. Fire beat them back, the heat so intense that it threatened to burn lungs and scorch flesh.

He had a vague sense of disbelief, a feeling of betrayal when with a crash, the third-floor roof groaned and then fell in on them. Holding Elizabeth and Sarah close, the three disappeared in a cloud of smoke and burning timbers.

Chapter 30
Present

As Nicole went through her bedtime routine, the history of the hotel and the cast of ghostly characters played through her head. It all started the first night with her chance encounter with the cowboy. He could have easily stepped straight from the silver screen of a classic western movie to the hallway. Ruggedly handsome, streaked with dust, sporting jawline stubble, he looked like a man who had never backed away from a fight.

Later that night, the ghost tour confirmed for her the tales of paranormal activity were not exaggerated. The phenomena of flying orbs in the ballroom, the sudden cold spot on the third floor, and the crazy beeping and flashing of the EMF meter outside her room reinforced the feeling spirits of the dead were definitely at work in the historic establishment.

Washing her face and brushing her teeth, she caught herself listening constantly for sounds of—well, anything. Extremely aware, she quickly glanced around the room, checking for anything out of place. She warily eyed the mahogany wardrobe in one corner. *Just the kind of place something or someone would hide,* she thought.

Hair brushed, PJs on, Nicole scooted on hands and knees to the middle of the bed she shared with Kat, feet tucked up under so no monsters of the night could grab her ankles. She reached for the lamp and switched it off but refused to crawl under the covers and close her eyes.

Nicole plumped the pillows at her back and reined in her runaway imagination while remaining vigilant, determined to stay awake until Kat and Mariah returned. But gradually drowsiness crept in. She struggled with eyelids that became heavier and heavier the longer she waited. She tried to fight it, but finally, lashes fluttered, and she drifted in and out of sleep.

Gentle taps at her shoulder roused Nicole. She struggled to open her eyes. The clock on the bedside table read 12:00 midnight. Thinking it was Kat pestering her, she said, "Leave me alone." No sooner had she closed her eyes and started to drift off again the taps came more forceful and insistent.

In the silence of the darkened room, she sensed an unearthly presence. She knew instantly it was him—the cowboy. She felt the soft breathing just above her. As he inhaled and exhaled, she fought the urge to begin breathing in unison with him. The next moment she felt a touch on her forehead, light, soft, like the touch of lips. There was a momentary pause, then a slow sigh. He lay his head next to hers on the pillow and whispered his name softly in her ear, "Tanner... Tanner."

Ghosts of Perry House

She jerked straight up when a jarring clang-clang-clang of metal on metal sounded from the foot of the iron bedstead. A shiver raced through Nicole like an electric current. Sapphire eyes, wide open, darted from dark corner to dark corner of the empty room.

Blonde hair swirled as her head swiveled to the bank of windows overlooking the park. Golden flames flashed into existence. Leaping and twisting into a fiery dance. Flares of color shot from the floor, licking the ceiling, devouring everything in their path. Then the monster of red, orange, and yellow disappeared as quickly as it had appeared, plunging the room into darkness once again.

Hoping it was all a dream, she shut her eyes and reopened them. Jumping to her feet, she whirled in circles, peering into every suspected secret hiding place. "This is not real... this is not really happening."

She froze in place as a voice from the hall screamed, "Fire!" The sounds of chaos erupting on the other side of the wall propelled Nicole into action. Not knowing what she would find, she yanked the door open and ran from the room certain she was headed for a midnight rendezvous with the ghostly spirits of the 1905 Basin Park Hotel.

Bewildered, she found herself alone in the middle of the third floor. Was it fear that created this dream world where the cowboy resided? They say dreams are an accumulation of what happens during the day. Had the stress and anxiety brought on by the card reading and the warning by Juliana Fay disrupted her thoughts and perceptions making it difficult for her to recognize what was real and what wasn't?

Yes, she was frightened and confused. But she wasn't crazy.

Without warning, the floorboards behind her creaked with heavy footfall. Before she could move aside, something rushed along the passage where she stood, it was, racing madly at full speed.

Close behind, came the pounding tread of more feet. The floor shook. Nicole just had time to flatten against the wall when the jumble of flying steps was upon her, with the slightest possible interval between them, they dashed past at full speed. It was the perfect whirlwind of sound breaking in upon the midnight silence in the empty hallway. Yet, she had seen absolutely nothing.

At that moment there came a terrifying crash in the corridor at her back. It was instantly followed by shrill, agonizing screams... cries of terror and cries for help melted into one. Turning, she found only a hallway, darkened with shadows.

Nicole's insides turned cold, hardening, making it impossible for her to breathe. Somehow, she had crossed the barrier that divided the world of the living from the world of the dead and witnessed the sounds of a horrific tragedy. How and why? These were questions she would never be able to answer. It was certain to be a mystery that would plague her for the rest of her days.

She tried to scream, but there were only gurgling sounds in the back of her throat. Darkness crept over her, taking away thought, taking away everything. She fell, the floor rising to meet her.

Kat and Mariah found Nicole crumpled on the floor outside room 310, looking dazed, eyes wide open as if fully awake but not seeing. Not responding to their questions, the two got her up and back in the room.

Chapter 31
Present

The moon shone bright white in the cloudless sky as the courtesy van wove a path along the narrow, winding mountain street. The thick line of trees on both sides formed a canopy. The moonlight filtered through the leaf-covered branches, casting ominous shadows, adding a dark foreboding feel to their escape.

The desk clerk was not unsympathetic to the plight of the three-guests, experiencing unusual activity in room 310, but she was unable to transfer them to another room. The hotel was fully booked for the weekend. The manager, heading off a public relations crisis, stepped in and came up with a satisfactory solution. And within minutes, Kat, Nicole, and Mariah were packed up and on their way to the Basin's sister hotel the Crescent just a few miles up the mountainside.

Wedged in-between her sister and friend, Nicole stared straight ahead. She had no idea what to make of the last hour. Was it a dream? A dream is a dream, but the feeling it left on her felt more real than something that was merely in a dream. Kat insisted she had been sleepwalking. "Remember, it happened all the time when we were kids. Mom would find you up and walking around the house late at night with a glazed, glassy-eyed expression just like a zombie."

"Yes, but I outgrew it by the time I was a teenager," Nicole protested. No matter what Kat said, Nicole wasn't convinced. It wasn't a dream, and she hadn't been sleepwalking.

Nicole decided to speak up, "I think the Ghost Whisperer was right. The boundaries separating the world of the

Ghosts of Perry House

living from the world of the dead are blurred at the Basin Park Hotel, allowing spirits to pass through some sort of opening to our world."

Mariah suggested, "More like a gateway or... doorway."

"Ok, let me see if I have this straight," Kat stopped, taking a deep breath, she turned in her seat, looked around Nicole, and faced Mariah. "You're telling me that the hotel has some sort of supernatural doors, just like physical doors that allow a person to pass from inside to outside, these doors allow passage back and forth from a dimension that holds the spirits of the dead."

"You have a better explanation?" Mariah wanted to know. "Maybe one of the many scientific theories you are so fond of sharing with us of late?"

Irritated with Kat for trying to explain away everything that had happened over the last couple of days, Mariah put forth her own theory, one her grandmother had shared before her passing. "What if—people who have crossed over do have access to our world. That would mean they can not only communicate across dimensions but also can make their presence known to us in ways that appeal to all our senses."

Taking a moment to get her thoughts in order, Nicole finally said, "So, the balls of light captured in the Barefoot Ballroom, the voices and sounds in the hallway, and my encounters with the cowboy can all be attributed to the spirit world wanting to make contact with me? But why?" Nicole asked as the van rounded a curve and turned onto Prospect Avenue revealing their destination.

The courtesy car slow-rolled the last few feet of the avenue, showcasing the spectacular beauty of the resort. Beyond the torchlight of the Victorian gardens, the magnificent hotel rose into the night sky atop the highest point of the mountain. The massive limestone structure towered above Eureka Springs like some ancient royal European castle overlooking its kingdom.

As the van came to a complete stop in front of the hotel, Mariah attempted to answer Nicole's questions, "Maybe it's as simple as not wanting to be forgotten."

Nicole mulled over what Mariah had said. "Yes, that has to be it. Unable to move on, trapped in a loop, reliving the tragic events of their death for eternity, they just want someone to know their story."

"You know what I think? I think you two are full of..."

The driver, quick to open the sliding van doors, interrupted Kat. Signaling for a bellhop, the luggage was unloaded onto a cart while he helped the passengers to the red carpet.

Standing in front of the vast, five-story limestone building, Mariah hesitated. Would she feel a chill as she entered? If she looked up, would she find a ghostly apparition staring down out of a window? Not chancing it, she dug for the buckeye buried in her pant pocket. Finally, latching on to it, she fell in behind Nicole and Kat.

The landscape lighting cast shadowy shapes on the surrounding surfaces as the three climbed the front steps. A stray gust of wind drifted down the empty drive, waking a monetary rustling of trees at their backs.

With a backward glance at the moonlit courtyard, the three guests passed into the grand foyer. The tiny sparkle cast by the hundreds of crystal dangling from the chandelier waltzed the room to the strains of an imaginary orchestra. As if propelled by an invisible hand, the enormous wood and glass doors slammed behind with a roar, echoing through the corridors and dark passages of the hotel.

The doorman greeted the trio, "Welcome to the 1886 Crescent Hotel and Spa, America's most haunted hotel."

Haunted Eureka Springs

Eureka Springs, Arkansas, is known as one of the most haunted towns in America. Visitors can experience the thrill of ghost hunting while staying at a real-life haunted hotel.

Haunted Hotels

The 1905 Basin Park Hotel openly promotes its haunted reputation. Many guests come to the Basin Park Hotel to experience firsthand the mysterious happenings reported by guests staying on the third.

The 1886 Crescent Hotel & Spa is one of the most well-known haunted hotels in America. Ghost sightings and stories are numerous and date back to 1885 during the construction of the hotel. In 2005, the Crescent Hotel was featured on the TV shows "Ghost Hunters" and "My Ghost Story."

Ghost Tours

The Basin Park Hotel Ghost Tour is conducted every Friday, Saturday, and Sunday night. The two guides for the tours are mediums. Aside from exploring the hotel, the tour also gives guests the haunted history of Eureka Springs and the hotel.

The Crescent Hotel Ghost Tour featured on numerous national television programs for its paranormal activities, offers multiple nightly ghost tours. Hear tales of "The Ghost in the Morgue" and the "Girl in the Mist." The tour ends with a visit to the creepy former hotel morgue.

The "Van Ghost Tour" takes visitors to several haunted locations including the catacomb of underground tunnels that traverse the town.

Ghosts of Perry House

The "Walking Ghost Tour" takes visitors downtown to two haunted locations ending in the underground tunnels.

"Ghost Stories in the Dark" offers ghostly tales told in the comfort of a hunted downtown location.

Attractions and Events

Intrigue Theatre presents an evening of entertainment by illusionist Sean-Paul and medium Juliana Fay. The pair captivates and amazes the audience with their magical performance.

"Downtown Underground Tour" offers visitors an opportunity to hear stories about the Eureka Springs' Wild West period and to explore the town's secret labyrinth-like network of underground tunnels.

Zombie Crawl is an annual event held the Saturday before Halloween. A parade of hungry zombies followed by doomsday floats and vehicles descend Spring Street to the Basin Park.

CC Brown

Voices from the Silent City is an annual event that takes place in October. Actors in period costumes take visitors on a guided tour of the Eureka Springs Municipal Cemetery while sharing stories of the unique and colorful history of the town.

Acknowledgments

We would like to express our appreciation to several people; for without their support and encouragement, this book would not have been written.

A special thanks to Bill Ott, former Director of Marketing and Communications for the 1886 Crescent Hotel and the 1905 Basin Park Hotel. We sincerely thank him for his support and helpful comments.

Our deepest gratitude to Sean-Paul and Juliane Fay of Intrigue Theater for taking an interest in our book and giving us helpful advice and recommendations. A visit to your theater is always the highlight of our trips to Eureka Springs.

Thank you to Debra Moen, Executive Director of the Eureka Springs Historical

Museum, for her invaluable assistance with our research of Eureka Springs. We are thankful to the museum board for giving us permission to use the Perry House photograph and for their willingness to preview chapters of the manuscript.

We would like to recognize Keith Scales, a tour guide with Basin Park Ghost Tours and the author of *House of a Hundred Rooms*. Keith has always been generous with his time and willingness to share his knowledge of writing and the history of the Basin Park Hotel. We appreciate his suggestions and insights.

Much gratitude to our good friend Janie Doss for once again taking on the challenge of proofing our manuscript. Her efforts definitely make G*hosts of Perry House* a better read.

We will forever be thankful to our friend, and sometimes writing partner, Carolyn Craig for editing portions of our manuscript. She is a relentless taskmaster: pushing us to do better, encouraging us to eliminate redundancy, and insisting we strive to improve dialogue between characters in order to make them "come alive."

A huge thank you to Phil Schmidt, the real-life inspiration for our fictional character, Tanner. Both men are fighters and survivors.

To our family and friends, we appreciate your never-ending encouragement and support, even though you do not share our fascination for spirits who reside on the "dark side."

Dark Side Series
Books by CC Brown

Black Widow Society

The sacred relic of the undead... *Vampire Bible* has fallen into the hands of a paranormal-artifact dealer Koleen O'Brien. An eBay bid and an annual vacation lead Koleen and her friends to San Antonio to deliver the book to a wealthy Texan. They are clueless to the fact that a pack of blood-thirsty vampires is stalking them to reclaim the Bible. Immortals meet their match as they discover that these women aren't typical mortals, they're members of the Black Widow Society!

Wolf Stone

Just when Dimtri thought nothing could stop him from executing his plan to become king of the shapeshifters enters sexy Mona Dix. The sacred relic of the werewolf nation, the Wolf Stone, has fallen into her hands. With the possession of the stone comes the power to dominate and rule the thirteen werewolf tribes.

Vacationing on the Oregon coast in the rugged terrain of the redwood forest, Mona and her friends are unaware of Dmitri and the pack of ancient wolves in hot pursuit to retrieve the precious stone. For the first time, Dmitri meets a woman who is more than a match for his supernatural powers and strong will. She is a Black Widow and member of the "Society."

Wolf Stone
Available at Amazon.com

Chapter 1

The black wolf threw back his head filling his lungs. Each breath sent signals along the olfactory nerve to his brain. Detecting a trace of her musky essence, his nostrils quivered. Smells, more than sights or sounds, determined his direction. His lungs sucked in the trail of her fragrance, and he followed the tiny molecules of chemicals floating on the night air.

Danger! Beware! Mona was jolted from a silent, motionless sleep. What had awakened her? Engulfed in darkness, she sat straight up on the lower bunk and strained to locate the sound that had penetrated her sleep. The soft whooshing of Amtrak's Superliner over the tracks was the backdrop for other sounds, the muffled laughter, and whispered voices of the other passengers.

Certainly, no cause for alarm, no reason to panic, she assured herself.

Chilled, Mona eased back onto her pillow. She pulled the covers snuggly up to her chin and allowed the gentle swaying of the train to work its magic. Her body and mind, little by little, relaxed and floated toward sleep. As she drifted, twisted images she could not control flashed: last summer, Texas, and Sven.

She caught a fleeting glimpse of dozens of riverside cafes and bistros lining the River Walk one story beneath the streets of San Antonio. Tourists strolled the winding walkways while a river cruiser traversed the narrow canal under the twinkling lights reflecting off the water. Colorful umbrellas adorned outdoor patios stretching to the river's edge creating an infectious air of celebration.

As if viewing the festive scene through

the long tube of a rotating kaleidoscope, the images shifted, creating multi-colored patterns that swirled faster and faster as if controlled by an invisible hand until at last all the colors blended into an inky blackness. Out of the darkness and into her thoughts stepped Sven. Sexy and dangerous, he was a vampire with a voracious hunger. He had kidnapped her from the River Walk turning her holiday into "The True Adventures of Mona Dix: A Texas Horror Story!" She had been held captive for days, serving as Sven's personal blood bank.

As she slipped into oblivion, just before the moment where all thoughts faded into the nothingness of slumber, Mona touched her neck reliving the pain and pleasure of the sharp pinch at her throat and the raging fire that burned deep inside as he fed.

A single, eerily haunting note rose sharply at first then broke, jerking Mona from the edge just before consciousness was completely lost to sleep. Heart pounding, eyes wide, she listened. A chorus of howls followed as others of its kind responded, each joining in at a different pitch. Wild, untamed music echoed through the night. Old and ancient as the earth, it spoke to Mona's dark side. Since her encounter with the rogue vampire and his blood-lusting brethren twelve months ago, Mona had changed. Her mind and body seemed to be tuned-in to the broadcast of unseen waves of vibrating energy aimed at her psychic center.

A quiver shivered up her spine. It wasn't a feeling of fear, but a tingling brought on by the excitement of something otherworldly. The animal cries tugged at Mona, luring her to the waist-to-ceiling picture window that stretched the length of the private compartment.

Compelled to investigate, Mona folded back the covers and slid her legs to the floor. She switched on the nightlight and surveyed the room. All the sleeping compartments were located on the upper level of the double-decker Superliner. At night, the rooms were dominated by two twin-sized bunk beds. During the day, the lower bunk could be transformed into two lounge chairs while the upper bunk could be folded into the wall and out of sight.

Mona had claimed the bottom bunk. She peered at her friend, Dominic, in the upper. Dead to the world, she thought.

Mona slid the curtain back and watched the landscape sweep by in slow motion. The moon, nearly full and bright, hung in the night sky bathing Glacier National Park in a faint golden haze. The Amtrak brochure had billed the preserve as "two thousand square miles of some of the most beautiful and dramatic natural scenery on the North American continent." The multi-hued summits and peaks of the northern Rocky Mountains rose steeply from the gently rolling plain. The forested valley at the base of the mountains opened onto a grassy meadow.

Naked, Mona stood looking through the window. She refused to hassle with nightgowns. Mocha brown, gypsy hair cascaded down her back and spilled over her bare fleshy shoulders. One of her lovers described her as Rubenesque: beautiful, sensual, and voluptuous. A knowing smile tugged at the corner of her lips; curves were sexy... magical. When a man sees a woman with curves it's like someone has injected him with some kind of drug that erases all logical thought and replaces it with a type of euphoric longing. Her philosophy: guys liked a little junk in the trunk; only dogs wanted bones.

Framed in the moonlight filtering through the glass, she searched the night. Her fingers absently sought the glassy-black stone carving dangling from the delicate gold chain around her neck. She found caressing the cool smoothness of the surface between her finger and thumb oddly comforting. Her gaze was drawn to a shadowy silhouette keeping pace with the train. As Mona observed, the outline became more defined. It took the shape of what appeared to be an extremely large dog. Maybe a German shepherd, she thought. It had no trouble keeping pace with the train. Loping along with ease, its body appeared to float over the rough terrain bordering the track. The movement of its strong muscles and long legs were relentless and effortless.

The animal drew near the window, mouth slightly open, large oversized white fangs exposed. Mona stood frozen as it turned up its nose, sniffed the air, and directed its stare at her.

A wolf—a very massive, black wolf—with red glowing eyes! Mesmerized, she was unable to look away. Gazes now locked; Mona got the distinct impression that the beast was trying to communicate. What was it? An invitation? A warning? No, that's crazy! she thought.

The wolf suddenly broke its hold on Mona and loped off across the grassy plain. She detected others of its kind. Shadows within the shadows of the pines, they waited at the edge of the forest. Watchful, they focused on their leader heading for a herd of grazing elk. Ready to combine their strength and cunning, they joined the hunt.

Mona moved from one side to the other of the window straining to get a better view of the chase. She pressed her face to the glass and positioned her hands on each side of her head blocking out everything except the dark shapes approaching the herd. She watched in fascination then horror as the wolves coordinated their attack with the precision of a military operation. With the fluid motion of long distant hunters, they quickly singled out and separated their chosen prey.

Squinting, she could barely make out the pack running along both sides of the elk. Heart hammering, violent shivers rocked Mona as she became the sole witness to the vicious assault. The kill was swift; the defenseless elk fell and lay sprawled on the ground.

An avid conservationist, Mona was aware of the nature of death. The cycle of birth and death was vital for survival in the wild. Cruel as it might seem, the drama she had just witnessed was one phase of the cycle. She understood violence was part of nature, part of the world in which animals live, and part of a natural balance.

Mona's last image as the train sped into the night was the black wolf slashing the elk's belly with jaws of steel. Before he feasted, even from the long distance, his red orbs once more pinned Mona. Razor-sharp incisors tore a hunk from the fresh-kill; he swallowed it whole. Mona came to the terrifying realization that the slaughter had been for her benefit. That's when the screams began.

Made in the USA
Middletown, DE
16 June 2021